ANN KELLEY is a photographer and prize-winning poet who once nearly played cricket for Cornwall. She has previously published collections of photographs and poems, an audio book of cat stories, and some children's fiction, including the award-winning Gussie series. She lives with her second husband and several cats on the edge of a cliff in Cornwall where they have survived a flood, a landslip, a lightning strike and the roof blowing off. She runs courses for aspiring poets at her home, writing courses for medics and medical students, and speaks about her poetry therapy work with patients at medical conferences.

By the same author:

Inchworm, Luath Press, 2008 (a novel)
The Bower Bird, Luath Press, 2007 (a novel)
Because We Have Reached That Place, Oversteps Books, 2006 (poems)
The Burying Beetle, Luath Press, 2005 (a novel)
Sea Front, Truran, 2005 (photographs)
Paper Whites, London Magazine Editions, 2001 (poems and photographs)
The Poetry Remedy, Patten Press, 1999
Nine Lives, Halsgrove, 1998 (audio book, stories)
Born and Bred, Cornwall Books, 1988 (photographs)

A Snail's Broken Shell

ANN KELLEY

Luath Press Limited

EDINBURGH

www.luath.co.uk

First published 2010

ISBN: 978-1-906817-40-4

The author's right to be identified as author of this book
under the Copyright, Designs and Patents Act 1988 has been asserted.

The publisher acknowledges the support of

 Scottish
Arts Council

towards the publication of this volume.

The paper and board used in this paperback are
natural recyclable products made from wood grown in
sustainable forests. The manufacturing processes conform to the
environmental regulations of the country of origin.

Printed in the UK by
JF Print, Sparkford

Typeset in 11 point Sabon

To Dr Kate Dalziel, with thanks

'The flowers of life come to everyone.
One has to be ready not to miss them.'
Compay Segundo

Fairy Godmother

Forgive me if I do not bestow
the usual gifts of riches and beauty.

I would rather grant stillness in your life
for regarding small things:

the angle of a wren's tail, for example,
or the slow flowering of lichen,

a quietness in your heart
allowing you to notice snowdrops

lighting the darkness under an apple tree,
how at 4pm on the last day of January

wet sand is the blue of a robin's egg,
how a single bluebell has no smell

but a bluebell wood has a cold fragrance,
how an olive leaf is like a silver fish,

and a severed cypress bract
is the green foot of a hummingbird.

May you be watched over
by the god of simplicity –

a piece of smooth beach glass,
an ermine moth on muslin,

a god who brings joy at the sight of a daisied meadow,
who shows one palm leaf waving while others are still,

and offers calmness
to watch the healing of a snail's broken shell.

PROLOGUE

DARK CLOUDS SHROUD the hills of Camborne and Redruth, but the little town of St Ives is bathed in bright light. The white, huddled houses, the orange roofs and the pale harbour beach shine like a beacon showing me the way home.

CHAPTER ONE

MARCH 2000. I breathe in the clean, sweet air, filling my new lungs with the familiar smell of home.

'Don't worry, puss, we're nearly there,' I whisper to Bubba, as Alistair drives us up Barnoon Hill. She's been so good on the long journey, and was a great hit on the train, entertaining children and charming the ticket man, who very kindly didn't charge us for her.

'Go in, I'll bring the luggage,' Alistair tells us.

Mum unlocks the back door and we go in.

Flo and Charlie are on the stairs, looking down between the rails.

'Charlie! Flo-Flo!' I put down the pet carrier and go to stroke them. Charlie mews loudly and Flo runs away up the stairs. Rambo's not to be seen – he'll be hiding under a bed. Charlie lollops upstairs with Flo, not sure if she should be welcoming or grumpy. I'm sure she's put on weight.

'Flo-ee, Flo-ee, Charlie!' Cats are generally unforgiving when you leave them to cope without you for just a day or so, and we've been away for nearly four months.

'Oh, so many daffodils!' Mum says. 'How lovely!'

The sitting room is yellow with flowers, as if the sun is shining from the room. They are on every surface, filling all our jugs and vases.

There's a knock on the back door.

'Come in, come in,' trills Mum. 'It's open.' And in comes Mrs Thomas from next door. She hugs us both, tears in her eyes.

'Oh, my dear, you look 'ansome, my girl.'

'I know,' I say. 'Look, I'm pink. And thank you so much for looking after our cats.'

'Back from the Darlings yesterday, they were,' says Mrs Thomas, dabbing at her eyes with her apron. 'They brought the flowers.'

'Lovely,' says Mum again, inhaling the cold smell of the petals. 'Oh look, Gussie, so many cards!'

> *Welcome home dearest Gussie!*
> *Love from Claire, Moss, Fay, Troy, Phaedra,*
> *and last but not least, Gabriel.*
> *Hugs and kisses, The Darlings **xxx***

There's a whole pile of cards. I search for Brett's handwriting, remove an envelope and put it in my pocket.

'I think the cats knew you were coming. Sat in the window all day, they 'ave.' Mrs Thomas absent-mindedly rubs at a mark on the table with the hem of her flowery apron.

'And how are your eyes?' Mum asks her. Mrs Thomas had cataracts removed while we were in London having *our* operations: Mum's emergency hysterectomy and my new heart and lungs.

'Perfect vision, my cheel. No problems at all. Can read the *Echo* and watch my programmes – it's marvellous. Now, before I forget, steak and kidney. It's in the Rayburn. Should be ready at six.'

'Oh, you shouldn't have,' says Mum, smiling. 'Stay and have some, Marigold.'

'No, my queen, I want to get back to my programme. I'll

see you tomorrow when you've both rested. Cats 'ave 'ad their tea.'

'Did I hear steak and kidney?' Alistair has taken the luggage up to our rooms and has come back down, rubbing his hands together.

'Let me shower and change first,' says Mum.

'It's okay, Lara, I'll do some potatoes,' says Alistair. 'I'll just park the car.'

'Potatoes is done,' says Mrs Thomas. 'What've you got there?' She points at the pet carrier, from which a squeak sounds.

'A kitten. Her mother abandoned her.'

'Another cat? Oh my soul!' She shakes her grey head solemnly and leaves without seeing the new kitten.

Should I get Beelzebub out and introduce her to the other cats or leave her downstairs and go to make peace with them first? She's mewing and might need a wee. I lift her out of the cardboard box and cuddle her. Her eyes, blue until a week ago, have changed now to a daffodil yellow. Perhaps I should have called her Daffodil. But my new kitten is coal black, even her whiskers and paw pads, and the name Beelzebub suits her very well. She was a little devil when we were staying at Daddy's flat in London, ruining his suede sofa and the black mosquito net over his bed. Her claws are needle-sharp.

I show her the water bowl and the leftover cat food. She laps at the water but isn't interested in biscuits. She's more interested in exploring her new home. I show her the inside loo – Rambo's litter tray – and leave her to find her way around the downstairs rooms before I go to my room. Cats are very independent and need to explore new territory completely. So they know where they are.

I can climb all the way up to the attic room without

stopping several times to get my breath. I feel like Superman – Superwoman, rather. Before I had my transplant I could hardly get to the first floor without having to sit on a stair for several minutes before carrying on. It was like mountaineering in thin air. My lungs and heart were so badly diseased that even crossing a room made me breathless and dizzy.

From my room at the top of the house I see right over the town and harbour, Smeaton's Pier, and to the far lighthouse at Godrevy and beyond. I see the weather coming at us from the horizon, the huge clouds building into orange and brown bouncy castles, squalls of rain like muslin curtains across the bay. A tiny slice of rainbow colours the sky to the west.

The cats are on my windowsill. Flo flies off in a huff, back and tail fluffed up, but Charlie mews and waves her tail and waits for me, looking confused and happy at the same time.

'Oh, Charlie, I've missed you so much.' I pick her up and she leans her head against mine, quiet at first. I whisper sweet nothings to her, she purrs. But she soon leaps down.

I tear open the envelope to find a card with an illustration of two swans, their heads touching, their necks making a heart shape.

> *Welcome home Gussie,*
> *See ya soon for some birding.*
> *Brett*

I look in the mirror and see what I suspected: my cheeks are rose pink from pleasure. Blue-grey was the usual hue, BT (before transplant). How strange that Brett should have chosen swans!

There are flowers in my room, too: a dense bunch of Paper Whites in a blue jug. They smell of spring and hope.

I unpack Rena Wooflie, smooth down her checked dress, put her on my bed, and sit on the striped cushion to gaze out at the gulls on the roof. Two mature gulls, a large handsome male and a trim female, stand and preen, their feathers quivering in the wind. The town looks just the same, except that there's scaffolding and polythene shrouding a few buildings on the harbour and on the opposite hillside. Building going on all over town.

I unpack my clothes, putting the dirties in a pile to go downstairs to the linen basket.

I look under my bed and yes, it's Rambo, curled up pretending to be asleep. I lie on the floor on my right side – the left side is still rather sore – and stroke the shy tabby.

'Poor Rambo, did you miss me? I'm sorry we've been away so long.' He purrs loudly, opens his big amber eyes and gazes lovingly at me. He's so forgiving.

'Gussie, come and see!'

'Come and see the new kitten, Rambo,' I whisper, and slowly stand up. 'What's the matter?' I shout down to Mum.

I practically fly down the stairs. Oh, it's so wonderful to feel so energetic. I still can't believe the difference my transplant has made to the way I feel and breathe. This must be what it's like to be normal. If it wasn't for all the drugs I have to take (only twice a day now, not five times as it was at first) and the various medical tests I have to record each day, and the monthly biopsies, I would be absolutely normal. Apart from the huge scar of course. But that's nothing to bother about. It's healed nicely, no more seeping. It's rather keloid: raised and red, and itches still, but that's a Small Price to Pay – as Mum says. If I hadn't had the transplant I would probably have died within the year.

'Nothing's wrong, darling. Look at that.'

Flo and Charlie are flat on their bellies peering under the sofa, ears back, tails flailing. Presumably Bubba's hiding from them.

'Oh no, they're in hunting mode.'

'They can't get at her, don't worry.'

'But she'll be terrified.'

'Come and have supper, Guss. She'll be all right. Let them get on with it,' says Mum.

Alistair, wearing Mum's blue apron, puts the pie-dish on a breadboard on the table and goes back to the kitchen for the mashed potatoes.

'Wasn't it thoughtful of Mrs Thomas to prepare our supper?'

'Mmm, smells good.' I have a ferocious appetite since my transplant. At first I lost my sense of smell, so food didn't taste of anything. But it's okay now.

Alistair has opened champagne and poured some for all of us. He's good at champagne – always finding occasions to open a bottle.

'New beginnings!'

'New beginnings!' we chorus, clinking glasses.

'And thank you to my donor.' I'll always be thankful to her and her family. I know it was a female under the age of twenty, but I don't know any more. Maybe the family will write to me, when the pain of losing their loved one has eased, but who knows when that might be? Maybe they'll never want to contact me. I could write to them of course, via the transplant centre, but I don't know what to say, except thank you.

We are all quiet for a moment, thinking of what might have been.

'Look!' The new kitten has appeared behind the other two cats, who are sitting with their front paws curled under them, eyes closed. Bubba sniffs the black and white fur of Charlie's huge bum. Her little black tail quivers in excitement. Flo opens her eyes and stares at the kitten. She doesn't move though, just watches with amazement. Flo is quite old – well, older than me, so about thirteen, which is old for a cat, and hasn't seen a kitten since Charlie was introduced to her, which was when I was ten. Bubba is patting Charlie's bottom, and Charlie's fur twitches. She turns suddenly and seeing Bubba, leaps backwards in surprise and takes off out of the room, followed closely by Flo, tail fluffed up again. They tear up the stairs, falling over themselves in terror of the tiny black kitten.

We all laugh. Bubba goes to the open door and goes to follow them. I don't think she can make the steep stairs and I get up to help her.

'They'll sort themselves out. Eat your nice pie before it gets cold.'

I watch my mother and Alistair. They can't stop smiling at each other. He's looking at her as if he loves her, even though she is fifty-two and is pale and thinner since her hysterectomy. I think she looks old and plain but he doesn't seem to notice. They laugh and chat and I'm content to daydream and eat.

CHAPTER TWO

THE SUN ON my face wakes me – that, or Charlie mewing at
the door. I let her in and get back into bed but keep my hands
over my chest so she doesn't step on my tender scar. She's
so pleased to see me. Flo is here too, sitting on the bedside
table, trying to look cheerful. She usually looks cross, as she
has black blobs each side of her nose by her eyes, which
give her a permanently bad-tempered expression, but this
morning she's purring. Where's Bubba? Have you eaten her?
I ask Flo, and she smiles. Oh dear, I hope she hasn't.

Beelzebub, or Bubba as I call her when she's good, was
playing on her own last night, chasing a toy mouse, the two
older females sitting high up out of her way on the sofa
back, staring with disgust at this tiny intruder. Then in came
Rambo, swishing his handsome tail like he does all the time,
even when he's pleased, saw the kitten, squinted at her, and
solemnly sniffed her all over. She cringed from him, ears flat
on her skull, back arched. Then he started to lick her tiny
head with firm slow licks until she relaxed. He licked her
all over, and then curled up with her to sleep on the rug.
Just like that. He's adopted her. The other two ignored them
both, or pretended to. I bet they're really fascinated though.
A new kitten for Flo to bully, a companion perhaps for
Charlie, and a surrogate daughter for dear old Rambo, who
has always been treated with disdain by the two females.

Can a cat be an underdog? Or last in the pecking order? Mixed metaphors, I think.

I have to have my pills now and wait an hour before I have my breakfast. There's no eating one hour before or one hour after the tabs. It's a drag, but part of my PT (Post Transplant) regime. No probs, as Brett would say. I look at his card again. The loving swans. Swans mate for life and if one dies the other never mates again. I wonder if it's a message. A sign of his undying love? Some hopes!

Note: Mute Swan, Cygnus olor. Actually, they aren't without a voice – they hiss loudly. Because they were all once the property of the crown, and prized food, their wing tips were clipped on one side to prevent them from flying, and the bell-beat of their wings was virtually unknown in Britain for five hundred years. Mutes have mainly orange beaks, Whoopers and Bewick's have black bills with diagnostic patterns of yellow. Head on, the yellow of Bewicks forms a letter B, and the yellow of Whooper is a W. The semi-tame mute swan is known for its gentleness.

Bewick's swans' calls are high-pitched and musical; in concert, can suggest the 'baying of hounds'. Whooper swans make a 'whoop-a' call, and so the name. It sounds honking and goose-like, a bit like a trumpet or a child's musical bicycle horn. Whoopers have deep strong calls. Apparently a dying bird makes a prolonged 'final expiration of air from the convoluted wind-pipe, producing a wailing flute-like sound given out quite slowly', hence the myth of the swansong.

And here's a quote from Cicero:

Death darkens his eyes and unplumes his wings,
Yet the sweetest song is the last he sings:

Live so, my love, that when death shall come,
Swan-like and sweet it may waft thee home.

I have decided to write nature notes in my journal between
pills and breakfast to stop me thinking about bacon and
eggs, sausage and baked beans, not that Mum ever cooks
all that. But we do go to the Cinema Café for a Full English
sometimes.

I like it there. It's a microcosm of life in St Ives. Visitors
and locals packed close together, and the family that runs the
place – gran, mum, daughter – cooking, serving, chatting,
laughing, arguing. And a little one, chirping like a sparrow
to the customers. And sometimes, at the outside table, a
bearded handsome man, who looks like a pirate, with a
handsome, bearded dog.

Note: 23 March 2000. Clouds build into massive grey hippos.
The roof gulls bicker – one pecking at another's wing as it
takes off. So sneaky.
  Mum had a letter from the council yesterday that stated
that our roof gulls have had no eggs for the last three years,
so they won't be coming to prick the eggs. Mum thinks there
is a ménage à trois – whatever that is. I think it means that
the gulls are just good friends. But, actually, there is nest
building going on. If you can call it a nest – a few twigs and
bits of moss from the gutters.

I read for a while then go down to find Mum drinking coffee
with Alistair.
  'Fed the cats?' I accuse her.
  'Yeah, yeah.'
  'And Bubba?'
  'Yes, Gussie.' She's in her tatty, tartan dressing gown. Her

hair is dishevelled and fluffy and she has bags under her eyes. Alistair must have stayed the night. I don't mind; I'm broad-minded. I realised when we were in London at Daddy's, that Mum and Daddy weren't going to get together again. He's too young for her for a start. Mum says he's a Peter Pan; he'll never grow up. Alistair's also younger than her, but then any single man would be – she's in her fifties. She had me when she was forty-one. But Alistair's more mature than Daddy. Because he's a doctor. You have to be serious if you are a doctor. Except that once I saw a movie about an American doctor called Patch Adams who was a clown and made children laugh. He ran a free hospital in New York, I think.

Medical care in America is not free. You have to pay lots of money for treatment. And if you are poor you don't get cared for. Even if you have medical insurance you only get a small amount of the care that you get here without paying for it. I saw a film about it. If you have cancer they won't pay for expensive drugs, they charge you extra. You get nice rooms though.

To get back to Daddy. Mum says that Daddy was unable to cope with my illness when I was a baby, and escaped whenever he could, travelling for work – he's a film archivist. I screamed a lot. She couldn't escape and says she seriously thought about strangling me or putting a pillow over my face, so she could sleep. Even if she'd been sent to prison she would've been able to sleep, she said. And if I ever did sleep, she thought I was dead.

She says that one night she woke with a shock to hear no screams and she thought I was probably dead, and she went back to sleep, because she knew that if she looked and I was dead, she wouldn't be able to sleep the rest of the night. She'd have to phone for a doctor, and start being distraught, and the need for sleep was the most important thing in her life at that moment. There was plenty of time to be distraught in the morning.

I think women should only have babies when they are young enough to stay awake all night and not mind. If they can dance all night then they can look after a baby that doesn't sleep. Perhaps she should have tried dancing with me, maybe then I would have slept.

'Mum, did you dance with me when I screamed in the night when I was a baby?'

'Did I what? Don't remember. It's all a Dreadful Haze, Gussie. I've blocked it from my mind. Eat your porridge. Wait. What time did you take your medication?'

'S'orright, Mum, I know what to do by now.' I sit at the table with my dish of porridge, spoon in a little runny honey and some yoghurt and eat. 'Alistair?'

'Mmm?' He is in his weekend clothes, not his suit, and is without a tie, for once.

'Did Mum tell you about my exhibition?'

'Exhibition? No, Gussie, what exhibition's that?'

'Daddy's organising an exhibition of photographs. Mine and my great-grandfather's.'

'Jeepers! That's wonderful! Well done Gussie.'

'I'll believe it…'

'When I see it.' I finish it for her. She doesn't trust Daddy to do what he's promised. But he won't let me down. It would be too hurtful of him. I know he's let me down in the past, but this exhibition was his idea, not mine, and he is enthusiastic about it. I've seen some of the huge black and white prints of images I'd made of the old men in the fishermen's lodges, and the staff in the transplant unit. He said they were good enough to exhibit. Good enough to be seen with a professional photographer's work. It's very exciting. I don't know why Mum can't be happy for me. Just because Daddy let her down, doesn't mean that he can't change. But she says, 'Don't hold your breath.'

Bubba is eating with the other cats, pushing in to have her share of the fish. She looks so little, her ears flattened so's not to touch the others. Rambo is, as usual, holding back until the females have finished. He's always known his place. Flo comes first, then Charlie, then Rambo. But Bubba doesn't know that. Suddenly Flo flies out at her, knocking her off her little legs.

'Oh, Flo, how could you?'

'Leave them, Guss. They'll work things out.'

Beelzebub cowers, going into reverse, and bumps into Rambo, who licks her protectively. She'll be all right.

'Flo – don't push it, don't push it, or I'll give you a war you won't believe.' I say in a threatening voice to Flo, who ignores me.

'What did you say?'

'Don't push it, don't...'

'Yes, but...?'

'Rambo, *First Blood*. Rambo said that when...'

'Movie mad! How can I have brought such an eccentric child into the world?'

'Rambo. A tad violent, I'd have thought, for a twelve-year-old?'

'Oh, blame her father. He gives her all these Awful Movies.'

'They're classics. Classics! You have to see the classics.' I shout.

'Yes, all right. Don't be so loud. We're not deaf. Now go have your bath, there's a good girl.'

'Can I finish my breakfast first?'

'May I, and Please.'

'Please may I finish my breakfast first?'

'Just do it quietly.'

She's got a hangover, I can tell. She hasn't removed her mascara from last night and it's in sooty splodges under her eyes.

Alistair winks at me, smiles at Mum, kisses her on the head and leaves with three big shopping bags.

'I'll be back,' he says, in a very good Arnold Schwarzenegger impression.

He's catching on.

CHAPTER THREE

'How I detest the dawn! The grass always looks like it's been out all night.' Lucille Ball, *The Dark Corner,* 1946

I AM TRYING to use a relevant film quote each day. This one is apt, as the long grass is still dewy and Bubba is getting wet. I'm sitting on a cushion on the step outside the front door, watching Bubba explore the garden. It's windy but bright and sunny. I have remembered to put sunscreen on. I'll have to do it from now on, even in the winter, because transplant patients are prone to skin cancers. That reminds me of a conversation I overheard when I was with Mum in a pub garden. This man said to the waitress, 'My wife is prone to white wine.'

Rambo's litter tray is put outside in the daytime, and she has already used it. (Bubba, not Mum or the pub wife.) The other cats aren't around. Rambo never goes out anyway, he's scared of the wildlife, and the two females are probably on my bed.

So Bubba is on her own in the big jungle, with what must look, to a kitten, like pterodactyls screaming overhead. She ignores them. Instead she's stalking a beetle. I don't think much of the beetle's chances. Yep, she's got him. Yum.

The gulls are already claiming territory ready for nesting on the roofs. The male on our roof has a particularly piercing scream. It must intimidate other male gulls though, because it works. He and Mrs Gull are on the lichened tiles, preening and making love. The same thing is happening on most of the rooftops. On a flat roof close by a pair of black-backed gulls have made their nest. They're even bigger than herring gulls and are their sworn enemies. They steal herring gull chicks if they get a chance and swallow them whole. But here they are close neighbours. And on the roof of the house in front there's a pair of jackdaws.

Bubba doesn't give a hoot about what is happening up there, she's too fascinated by the scents in the garden. I wonder if she can sense Shandy's ghost?

Mrs Thomas's cat, Shandy, died when Mum and I were in London having our operations, but I expect there are still wafts of his scent in the bushes. I must remember to say how sorry I am when I see her. I forgot yesterday. Not only is she a widow, she's lost her only cat too. Poor Marigold. I do like that name. My name is horrible – Augusta – Ugh!

A bee has landed on my knee and is carefully performing his toilet, nearly balancing on his nose to get the correct angle for washing his bottom with his back legs. Now he's washing his face and head with his front legs. I like insects almost more than I like birds. They're so extraordinary and there's so many of them. I like spiders too, and bugs. Most people think that insects and bugs are the same thing, but it's not so. Bugs have mouthparts that suck. What I mean is – sucking mouthparts that come out of the top of their heads. Bugs are from the Hemiptera family. They suck the life out of their prey.

I'm going to do an ecological survey of this garden. Perhaps Mrs Thomas would let me do it in hers. There might be completely different species in the two plots, even though they are next to each other. Our gardens are very small, about four metres by five. Ours has a cherry tree and an apple tree and short grass, and Mrs Thomas's has very long grass and a broken wooden bench and some straggly bushes.

Ours has a metal tree where we hang bird-feeders, and a bird-table, so we get lots of little birds: greenfinches, blue-tits, great tits, starlings, sparrows, song thrushes, missel thrushes, chaffinches, blackbirds, and even jackdaws and doves. Herring gulls land in the garden sometimes to scavenge bread or cheese that we've thrown out. I'm going to keep a record of them all. I'll start straight away. No time like the present – as my grandpop used to say.

Anyway, there might not be a tomorrow.

I keep forgetting that I've had a heart and lung transplant. Instead of only a year or so to live, I can look forward to maybe twenty years. It's hard to take in. I've always lived for the day. *Carpe diem* – seize the day. I can actually plan for the future. Unless something goes wrong.

CHAPTER FOUR

IT'S TIME I wrote the letter:

'*Dear donor family, I can't thank you enough…*' No, too formal.

'*Dear family of the donor who gave me my new heart and lungs, I can't begin to understand what you must be going through, having lost a loved one…*' No, too old-fashioned and cold. I must try to use my own voice:

Dear Family,

I am sorry for your terrible loss. I would like you to know that my new heart and lungs have given me hope for a healthy normal life. I'm nearly thirteen and will soon be back at school for the first time in over a year.

I can run again and breathe deeply. The transplant was successful, so far, though I have to go for check-ups and take immunosuppressants of course, but that's a small price to pay.

I want to thank you so much for my wonderful new life. I wish I could meet you to thank you properly, and I would love to know something about your loved one who died.

But of course I understand if you don't want to say anything to me or write.

Yours sincerely,
A very grateful recipient

PS *In a way I think of you as a part of me, because a part of me was part of your family.*

Mum says it's okay but I'm not to expect an answer. She sent it to the hospital transplant co-ordinator in an unsealed envelope with my full name and date of transplant. That's the correct procedure. I'm not allowed to give my name or address.

I don't suppose I can count the birds that fly overhead as part of my garden survey, which is a shame. For example, a strong wind is pushing a cormorant high over the yellow roofs. Where is he going? They are usually skimming the sea, not flying high. The tide is low and hundreds of gulls circle, chattering and chuckling, and land on the wet sand in large groups. On every roof-ridge gulls sit and look towards the sea. Jackdaws sit on the chimneys, in loving pairs. On the trellis of our garden wall a starling stands and peers into the garden. We've thrown out apple and pear cores and cheese rind. Blackbirds love those.

Flo has forgiven me for going away for such a long time. She's come to sit next to me, purring gently, occasionally gazing at me lovingly. She's going grey. Or rather, her black bits are speckled with white hairs. If it were Mum she'd dye them. I'm sure Mum had darker hair in old photos. She's getting blonder as she gets older.

It's a bit too peaceful, sitting here, cat-watching and bird-watching. I wish someone would call. Don't they know how lonely I've been? How ill? Why doesn't Brett call me? Has he found someone else to go birding with?

'Cup of tea, darling?' Mum hands me a mug of weak black tea, hardly coloured at all, just the way I like it, and a shortbread biscuit.

'What is it sweetheart?' She crouches to hug me.

I seem to be crying.

CHAPTER FIVE

'I'm going to be a lady if it kills me.' Jean Harlow,
Dinner at Eight, 1933

THE PHONE RINGS and Mum yells, 'For you, Gussie.'
 'For me?' I practically fall down the stairs.
 'Brett? Oh… oh, it's so good to hear your voice.'
 'Yeah, hi. Howyadoin?'
 'Good, I'm good.'
 'Can I see you? I mean, can I come over?'
 'Please do, yes, I mean, if you want.'
 'Orright. Be there in five.'
 'Brett?'
 'Yeah?'
 'Nothing. See you soon.'
 'Yeah.'

Ohmygod! Look at me. My face is puffy and spotty. It's the
drugs. I drag a comb through my hair and then gel it into
spikes. I go through Mum's make-up bag in the bathroom
and slap on some concealer. That's better. Make-up is magic.
Then I floss and brush my teeth.
 'Brett's here, Gussie.'
 'Hi. Get you, Guss. You're pink! You look great.'
 'Yeah, hi!'
 We do a high five, and I can't stop grinning. Brett looks

pretty pleased, too. He grabs me by the shoulders.

'Wow, you look… different.'

'I know.' I squirm in embarrassment. Have I put too much concealer on? Are my cheeks still hamsterish from the steroids? He looks just the same – blond, floppy, longish hair, his curly smile. He looks like a typical Aussie surfer, except that, unlike most Aussie boys, he isn't into sports. 'Thanks for the card,' I say.

'You up for some birding? Saw a great northern diver off the Island yesterday.'

'Oh yes, please. I mean, sure, okay, if you want.'

How come a gorgeous Aussie wants to go birding with me? Perhaps he needs glasses.

CHAPTER SIX

WE ARE LYING on tufted grass on the Porthmeor Beach side of the Island, looking through binoculars. It's not really an island, but that's its name. It's a grassy rocky peninsula where local women used to dry their bed linen in the old days. I've seen photographs, the sheets weighed down with stones. No one does that any more. They've got tumble dryers instead. But if we need to save fuel we should be hanging out our washing to dry in the fresh air.

That's what I'll do, I think. Make images of ordinary things. I'd like to do wildlife photography but it's too specialised and you need all sorts of expensive equipment, long lenses and heavy gear. I do have one long lens. But what might be seen as ordinary, everyday images to me might be of interest to someone else in the future, or from another country or culture. My normal 'dull' existence could be extraordinary and fascinating to someone far away.

I think of this as our special place. We sit side by side, a huge granite boulder behind us.

'Easter soon – a week with no school,' says Brett.

'Are you going away?'

'How do you…? What do you mean?'

'On holiday, going away?'

'Nah, staying here. Why go away when S'n' Ives is so good?'

We sit in companionable silence, listening to the waves

slapping the rocks, the tumult of gulls.

'What was it like, the transplant? Did it hurt?'

'They give you painkillers, so not really. But I had really scary nightmares afterwards – one of the drugs does that to you. That was the worst part. That and getting to like people who died.'

My eyes smart and my throat tightens. I don't know if I can talk about Precious yet. He died just before we came home to Cornwall. He was so beautiful. Like a pretty girl, but tall and strong. He was from Zimbabwe. He was gentle and had a soft whispering voice and he liked me lots. He had a lisp, so he called me 'Guthie', which always made me laugh.

I think I'm blushing but Brett's not looking at me. It's strange how transplant patients feel close to each other. As if we are in some exclusive club. It's difficult to explain to someone who has no idea of what's involved. Our transplants aren't cures. Instead, we have 'swapped death for a lifetime of medication'. That's a quote from one of the unit's leaflets.

'What's that?'

'Where?'

'Ten o'clock, waves.'

'A raft of weed?'

'Yeah, and something on it.'

'Ducks?'

'Could be diving ducks.'

'They're tiny. Must be dozens of them.'

'There they go.'

The flock take off and skim the waves, white wing tips catching the sun. Like a flutter of thrown confetti.

'Look them up, Guss.'

I thumb through the book.

'Buggering Nora, they all look the same to me.'

'Never mind. Like a mint?'

There's a smell of salty air and dry grass. A plastic kite shaped like two scarlet legs flies above us. Gulls squawk and nag.

'Look, a red kite!'

Brett laughs and slaps me on the back. I wince and he apologises.

'No worries,' I say. It's good to be home. 'With my brains and your looks, we could go places.'

Brett looks confused, or bemused, probably both.

'It's from a movie,' I explain. '*The Postman Always Rings Twice*.'

'Oh, righto!' he says, smiling his curly smile. I must capture that smile on film one day.

When I get back to the house there are messages for me. Bridget phoned to say she is shopping with her mum in St Ives this afternoon and she'll come round to see me. Claire phoned to say welcome home and to invite us to lunch tomorrow. She's popping in with Gabriel.

'Look at you!' Claire hugs me and Gabriel can't stop smiling. He has brought us some eggs from his Indian Running Ducks and a posy of primroses from their garden, which he shyly hands to me. They also have a box of home-grown vegetables and a loaf of bread baked that morning by Gabriel's dad, Moss.

Bubba is pleased to have so many people making a fuss of her. Charlie looks rather pissed off though, so I have to pick her up and cuddle her. But she escapes from my clutches and goes off in a fluffy huff.

Bridget arrives and she, Gabriel and I go upstairs to my room with Bubba. I still can't get over how much energy I have and how easy it is to climb stairs. I feel as if I'm flying.

Bridget has brought me a pot of tiny daffodils. She shoves pollen across my desk at me.

'Have some flower sperm,' she says.

'How's your puppy, Gabe?'

'Ace, geet ace. Couldn't bring her 'cos of your cats.'

'I don't think Bubba would mind, but I'm sure Charlie and Flo would hate her.'

'Are you going to start school, Gussie?'

'Yes, I think so, after the Easter hols. Can't wait.'

'I'd give a million pounds to get off school. I hate it,' says little Gabriel.

'So do I,' says Bridget.

'How's your sister?' I ask her. I don't really want to know, as I dislike Siobhan intensely. But maybe she's fallen down and broken one of her long legs, or her snub nose, or got her belly-button ring caught on a nail. That would be very satisfying.

'Gross, as usual.'

'No change there then,' I say, and we laugh. The kitten is walking along the windowsill watching the gulls on the roof. She hisses at them, her ears folded back on her head, her fur fluffed up. Now she's chittering crossly. She's so sweet. Gabriel goes to stroke her and she flicks her back at him. She's too busy being irate and fierce to be friendly.

Claire calls up, 'We're off now Gabriel. Come on.'

'But I've only just got here,' he moans.

'Come on before the fish shop closes.'

'Can't I stay?'

'No, come now.'

'Bye, Gabe, see you tomorrow,' I say and give him a hug.

'He's adorable,' I say to Bridget.

'Not at school he isn't,' she says. 'He's always in trouble. He spends most of his time outside the headmaster's door.'

'I don't believe it.' Gabriel can do no wrong in my eyes. His big sister Phaedra says he has a crush on me.

It's funny how we like people who like us. I suppose it's a bit like enjoying those subjects we are good at. Like English and Biology – my favourites. At least, they were, when I went to school. It's been such a long time, I might have become crap at lessons. If I don't go back soon, I'll have to have private tutors again. Brett's mum, Hayley is brilliant at teaching English – she brings poetry that I've never heard of, and I'm encouraged to write my own. I should probably be doing all sorts of things that are in the curriculum so I won't be behind when I do go back. Though I enjoy reading books about Zoology and Entomology and Ornithology. I'm probably all right with those subjects. She says I'm an 'autodidact'.

I decide to give all the cats a good combing, to get Bubba used to the idea of the daily routine. It goes like this: I bang on the garden table with the cat flea-comb and call the four cats, who jostle to be first in the queue. I give all my attention to Flo – the queen bee.

We've brought back loads of old movies from Dad's massive video collection. He gets to keep old copies that are about to be destroyed, even though they are perfectly okay. No horror movies. Mum won't let me watch them, though Daddy thinks I should be allowed to watch anything I want, within reason.

I think monster movies could use magnified images of real insects – like stag beetles or praying mantises – or is it 'manti'? They are as terrifying if not more than invented monsters. Real spiders magnified by a thousand would be really scary. Magnified ants are fearsome. I wasn't scared of

Mighty Joe Young or *King Kong*, but Mum thinks horror movies will give me nightmares. Alistair and Mum have gone out and Mrs Thomas is Gussie-sitting. Beelzebub has gone straight to Mrs Thomas and is curled up asleep on her lap.

'Do you miss your cat?' I ask her.

'Yes, my dear, I do. I think I hear him miaow sometimes and say – where're you to? Silly old girl I am. My Shandy was a great comfort. I'm still finding ginger hairs.'

'I don't know what I'd do if one of my cats died.'

Flo is the oldest cat – older than me but she has lots of energy and imagination. She's always chasing mice, even when they are pure fantasy. She'll stalk a piece of string, attack it, and carry it around, tossing it high and catching it again. She even brings it to me making a loud mew – the signal that she has caught something. It's the only sound she ever makes, apart from purring, unlike Charlie, who is demanding, nagging me to get out of bed and feed her, pushing her face into my hand when she wants to be stroked, crying at the bathroom door to come and join me.

'Shall we play Scrabble or watch a movie?' I ask.

'A film would be nice. What have you got, my flower?'

In the end we watch *The African Queen*, or rather, I do, and Marigold goes to sleep. I like to think of her as Marigold, because it's such a lovely name, but I know she prefers me to call her Mrs Thomas. It's more respectful. She calls me 'cheel' (Cornish for child) 'flower' or 'queen'. I do love it when I'm called 'flower'.

Watching *African Queen* makes me think of Africa, and the wonderful winters we had when I was little. Mum says you should never go back to places where you were happy because it's always a disappointment. But I would love to go back to Kenya and watch the vervet monkeys in the sausage trees, and go snorkelling. Not that *African Queen* has any snorkelling in it – just Humphrey Bogart wading through brown muddy river water full of leeches.

In bed I can't stop thinking about Precious. Why did he have to die? And then I start thinking about his hands, the colour of milky coffee on the back, the palms like a muddy African plain, dark creases like rivers flowing. And how large and warm his hands were when we danced – well sort of danced – on Hampstead Heath. And he said something lovely to me. He said we were like the swans on the pond, one black, one white, floating side by side.

If I hadn't had a congenital heart defect I wouldn't have had to come to Cornwall to get away from the pollution in London. And if I hadn't come to Cornwall I wouldn't have met Brett. And if I hadn't had a heart and lung transplant I wouldn't have met Precious. And if I hadn't met Precious – well, life would be less than it is. I wish he hadn't died but I'm glad I knew him, if only for a little while.

I have known many dead people: Grandpop and Grandma, several transplant patients at the hospital, Precious, and Shandy, except that Shandy was a cat, so he doesn't really count. But I know he counts to Mrs Thomas. He was her closest companion since her husband died.

I remember asking Grandma once, when I was little, if she was going to die. She said she'd never die. But she did. Maybe she meant that she would never die while I remember her. In my head she's there. And Grandpop. They'll always be there. And I'll never forget them. Precious too.

I read somewhere that our lives are like writing in the sand: everything we do and say and think will be washed away by the tide.

The night sea sighs. Darkness swallows a muslin moth.

CHAPTER SEVEN

BETWEEN THE MORNING medications and breakfast I make lists as well as nature notes. Film quotes:

'*Well, nobody's perfect.*' Joe E Brown as Osgood in *Some Like it Hot*, 1959. (When he hears that his fiancée, Daphne – Jack Lemmon – is a man.)

'*You don't understand. I coulda had class. I coulda been a contender. I coulda been somebody...*' Marlon Brando, *On the Waterfront*, 1954. (Brando in the back of an automobile, his arm muscles bulging in a white T-shirt. I'll have to watch it again to check.)

'*There's no place like home.*' Judy Garland, *The Wizard of Oz*, 1939. (I've only watched it recently for the second time. The first time I had to be removed from the cinema as my screams bothered the audience.)

'*Beulah, peel me a grape.*' Mae West, *I'm No Angel*, 1933 (I really must try and use that one next time Mum buys grapes.)

Why do sick people get grapes given to them in hospital? They must contain special minerals or vitamins that help with healing, I suppose.

Note: This morning is full of the promise of spring. In our garden the African bean tree is flowering and sparrows are chirping in it. Our roof gulls – five of them – are courting, fighting for territory and sleeping – not necessarily in that order. Flat-footed gulls pad about on the dormer roof. One stands on the roof window and I examine the red veins running through the webs of his feet. Four goldfinches take turns on the feeder. They love the sunflower seeds.

Mum and I are going for coffee on the harbour. Winter is ending and all the townspeople are smartening up their shops and cafés ready for the busy season. Ladders are propped up against slate-hung walls. Delivery vans park in the streets and cause traffic jams. A man with paint all over his overalls smiles at us and Mum throws back her hair and beams at him. I wish she wouldn't do that. Hasn't she heard about body language? Tossing her hair means she's interested in him, and she can't be, she's going out with Alistair. And I like Alistair.

She shouldn't flirt.

'Mu-um! I thought you liked Alistair?'

'So? It doesn't mean I'm totally immune to a bit of admiration. God, Gussie, you're worse than my mother. Do you know she wouldn't let me stay out after ten o'clock, Even when I was seventeen.'

'Well, I expect she thought that you'd get into trouble.'

'Well... yes.' Mum sips her coffee, looking thoughtful.

We sit outside in the sun.

'Can I have another slice of carrot cake?'

'May I and Please!'

'Please may I have another slice of carrot cake?'

'Yes, Gussie, of course you may. It's so Lovely to see you with an Appetite. I think you're putting on weight already.'

I'd forgotten we are going to lunch with the Darlings. But I'm sure I'll be hungry again in a couple of hours.

It'll be the Easter holidays soon. The town will be inundated with strangers, wandering along looking lost and as if they have all the time in the world. And the local people, who are in a hurry to finish their shopping, have to push past them in the narrow streets. It's so great to be actually living here and not on holiday. I don't have to go home in a week's time to some noisy, smelly city with nothing to look at except buildings and traffic and only a narrow sky and musty pigeons.

Here the air smells clean, we don't get smuts on our clothes, and there's so much to look at – the boats bobbing in the harbour, the big sky, the bay that changes colours all the time, the swooping, immaculate gulls. We hear the wind, the sea and gulls' cries, not snarling traffic and police sirens.

It's boring, having to deal with my anti-rejection drugs, and medical regime – the tests I have to do each day – weight, blood pressure, etc. I also have to remember when to take the vitamins and antibiotics. But it's all about habit. Once you get into a good habit, it becomes second nature; you forget about it. Like cleaning your teeth. How awful it would be if I could never clean my teeth again! Imagine if I had to go to bed with mossy teeth – yuk!

I have some bad habits – like biting my nails, leaving dirty clothes on the floor, and forgetting to light a match after I've been to the lavatory. A Grandma trick – you light a Swan Vesta to take away the pong. I do forget sometimes. But at least I open the window. I used to suck my right thumb, but I managed to give it up.

Mum says children should be allowed as much comfort as

they can get: a dummy, sucking a thumb, a cuddly blanket. I had all three. She has whisky and cigarettes, though she's given up smoking since my transplant. Maybe, now she's happy with Alistair and I've had my transplant, she'll not be as anxious as before and won't need the comfort of nicotine again. Wish Daddy could find someone to be happy with too. Find his perfect woman.

On the drive to the Darlings' house I spot a gull doing a rain dance on a grass verge. It looks so funny, a flat-footed tap dance. I've only ever seen thrushes doing that, to trick worms into thinking it was raining. They dance, then listen to the whisperings in the grass. Precious told me that there's a tribe in East Africa that love to eat white ants, and when there's a drought small boys are sent to dance on the hard dry earth so that the ants will think it's raining and come up to the surface.

Zennor runs barking towards us, wagging her shaggy tail. She has grown to be twice the size she was when last I saw her.

Gabriel is up his favourite tree, the one with a trellis of ropes and home-made platforms, a hanging rope, and a pulley with a basket for carrying tools and food. He's half monkey, Claire says. He prefers being in a tree to being earthbound. He is whistling away to himself, but stops to wave at us as we get out of the car, laden with drinks and cheeses. Perhaps he's part bird too.

'Come in, come in, it's a bit parky out there. Shame, it was so sunny earlier, really spring-like.' Claire ushers us into the house that Moss made with his own hands. Moss Darling is related to me via my Great-Aunt Fay, his mother, who is the daughter of my great-grandfather, the well-known Cornish photographer. So Gabriel, Phaedra and Troy are my half cousins or something like that. Family, anyway.

There's a wonderful spread. Warm savoury tarts, salads with bread freshly baked by Moss. He comes in from his workshop and hugs us both. Gabriel follows, looking bashful.

'Hands!' says Claire, and Gabriel follows Moss to the bathroom.

Phaedra appears, gorgeous under her fuzzy golden halo, the image of the portrait of her Grandmother Fay. Troy is out with mates.

'Is Fay here?' I ask Claire.

'Not yet. She's coming for Easter.'

'Where does she live when she's not in the cabin?'

'Devon. Totnes.'

'Oh. I've never been there.' I haven't been to many places in England apart from Essex and London and Cornwall. I've been to more foreign countries than English counties. One day I intend to go to America to see bald eagles and Australia to see cockatoos and New Zealand for the keas. I've seen them all at Paradise Park but I would like to see them in their natural habitat.

CHAPTER EIGHT

'Be afraid. Be very afraid!' Geena Davis, *The Fly,* 1986

WE'VE HAD THE most frightening storms over the last two days. March is good for gales – the spring equinox. Sand was hurled by the sea into the streets. Windows were smashed on harbour-front houses. Cars had to be moved from the Island car park as the sea was crashing onto them. Metal railings were torn up. A boat was ripped from its metal moorings on West Pier and thrown into the harbour. It ended up on the beach below the cliff where we used to live, two miles away. And there was a rogue wave, which would have lifted photographers and other storm watchers to their deaths, but police had just moved them away out of danger.

Sandbags lie like drowned pigs in every harbour-front doorway. There was a sea rescue in Penzance. Someone went down onto the beach after his glove and was swept out to sea. He was saved. Imagine nearly dying for a glove!

Two ships have been sheltering in the bay, plunging sickeningly into deep valleys and rising almost perpendicularly onto the peaks of waves.

I'd hate to be a sailor. My grandpop was a sailor. I wonder if he was ever seasick? I never asked him. So many things I should have asked him, but I thought he and Grandma would live forever.

We've been watching *Forrest Gump*. I thought it was sentimental but Mum cried lots. She likes movies that make her cry. I like movies that excite me and thrill me but make me think.

I hate predictable endings. And I hate movies where the heroine has to cut her own hair to disguise herself and it ends up looking brilliant (Judy Garland as Jo in *Little Women* cut her hair to sell it and it looked bloody awful, which is much more like reality). But Geena Davis and Angelina Jolie did it and their hair looked immaculate. And I hate in a movie when someone's driving a car and doesn't pay enough attention to the road ahead, but instead turns to look at the passenger all the time. You would crash if you did that in real life. And when someone hears a strange noise and they investigate, going down into a dark cellar on their own. No one would ever do that in real life.

Mum says I shouldn't say I hate things – it's too violent an emotion for a twelve-year-old. I've thought of another one – no one in horror movies draws the curtains or pulls down the blinds at night, and murderers can see them and get them. But in *Godfather 2* Kay says to Michael Corleone, 'Michael, why are the drapes open?' Cue mayhem and gunfire.

It's calm now, and foggy. A sea fret, a Cornish mizzle. The sea meets the sky in a uniform silver grey. The opposite hill where Tregenna Castle Hotel smugly sits is blanked out. It no longer exists. The mist drifts towards us in shreds.

There aren't many lights on yet: it's 6.15 and it's still daylight. Only the string of street lights on Tregenna Hill illuminate the gloom. Our roof gulls have flown off. The church clock is lit.

This room above the town, looking out over the bay, makes me feel light, airborne, like our roof gulls. My attic is a Gussie nest.

They're getting accustomed to me sitting up here, watching them. There were eight birds there today. All chatting and whispering sweet nothings to their mates. Flo chittered at them through the window glass, but the gulls walked by on the roof tiles, knowing they were safe from feline claws and teeth. I've opened the window a slit and Flo pokes her nose out, sniffing the deliciously fishy scent of *Larus argentatus* – herring gull. The sun stays last on the large flattish roof on the other side of the valley, and there are about a hundred gulls there. They are the sun-worshippers, the last gulls to leave town as night falls.

Jackdaws alight on our roof too. I wonder where they are going to nest. I must look in WH Hudson's book *The Land's End* to see if he mentions their nesting sites. I think there were probably more jackdaws than gulls on the roofs in his day. Herring gulls only started to use roofs as nesting places in the 1920s. He writes about jackdaws keeping warm on chimney tops. I wish I had known him. He was a sad man, a world traveller and naturalist from South America who died alone and penniless in Worthing, West Sussex.

In 1906 I found a lodging in a terrace rather high up, where I could look from my window at the bay over the tiled roofs of the old town. Here I had a front garden to feed the birds in, and better still, the entire jackdaw population of St Ives, living on the roofs as is their custom, were under my eyes and could be observed very comfortably. I discovered that they filled up a good deal of their vacant time each morning in visiting the chimneys from which smoke issued, just to inform themselves, as it seemed, what was being cooked for breakfast. This was their pastime, and watching them was mine. Numbers of daws would be seen, singly, in pairs, and in groups of three or four to half a dozen, sitting on the roofs all over the place. As the morning progressed and more and more chimneys sent out smoke, they would become active visiting the chimneys, where, perching on the rims, they would put their heads down to get the smell rising from the pot or frying pan on the fire below. If a bird remained long perched on a chimney-pot, his neighbours would quickly conclude that he had come upon a particularly interesting smell and rush off to share it with him. When the birds were too many there would be a struggle for places, and occasionally it happened that a puff of dense black smoke would drive them all off together.

Mum has made me a little silver plastic fish, like a sprat, which hangs above my bed and twists and turns in the air currents. It's shivering translucent in the air. There is a fish shadow, much bigger than the fish, on the ceiling. It's like I am looking down into a clear stream, seeing a live fish and its shadow on the riverbed. She's making lovely things. Not just her drawings, but three-dimensional things. She's set up a workbench in the spare room and I hear her hammering or sawing. She's producing a flock of painted seagulls made from thin wood. They stand on a block of wood and there's a peg on the back for holding postcards and invitations and notes. She's got golf tees for their noses. They look cross and funny.

Just thought of another movie hate: when the hero is always able to park right outside the building he needs to go in and leave it there. In my experience this never happens. Mum has to park in a car park two miles away and walk back. Sometimes, you really have to suspend disbelief at the movies. (Is that right? Or is it suspending belief? Let's try saying it another way – Don't believe everything you see in the movies.)

Mum has started attending jewellery-making classes with a local silversmith. She's keen to learn a new skill. I think she should give cookery classes to people – she's good at cooking interesting things, but she says she's not properly trained; she's only an amateur. I think she should write a book on how to cook with leftovers – vegetable and fish curries, fish soups, fish cakes and exotic salads. I'd help. I could do some photographs of the food. I've had a good idea – I'll make her a recipe book of her meals for her birthday.

Alistair is always complimentary about her cooking, but Mum says it's because he went to boarding school and the food was probably so awful, that anything is better than that. She says his palate has been institutionalised. First prep school, then public school, then university, then hospital. Nothing but canteen food. No wonder he likes Mum's cooking. Perhaps food is a consolation for life's troubles. I feel hungry all the time since my transplant. Especially when I'm unhappy. Like now. Maybe I should start cooking more.

CHAPTER NINE

I'M SITTING ON the front step. Mum's taken to watching Test Cricket on the telly in the morning and I'd rather sit in the sun. The granite step is very cold to my bare feet, though the sun is already warm. I'm so happy to be here. To have come through the transplant and to be feeling so well. I want to dance and sing loudly, like Doris Day in *Calamity Jane*. Strut and swagger in chamois leather trousers and boots and tote a gun. It's not my favourite musical, but I do like the character. My favourite musicals are the ones with Fred Astaire and Ginger Rogers in. All of them. And Gene Kelly in *Singing in the Rain*. *The King and I* was good too – *lurved* Yul Brynner's clothes. And *High Society*. Oh, to look like Grace Kelly! At least I'm pink now instead of blue grey. My eyesight is still poor, and my hair mousy, my limbs those of a stick-insect, but I am putting on weight and can do more exercise, and when I start school I'll be able to play tennis, rounders and maybe even cricket, like my grandma did.

Note: A bee bumbles in and out of the yellow flowers on the bush – don't know its name, but the shrub flowers all winter and looks like a small chrysanthemum. The council has planted them all along the roads into town. I don't like them much but bees do.

Sparrows are chirping in another garden along the terrace.

A starling struts on the path. They don't seem to be scared of my cats. They are more interested in the sunflower seeds in the bird-feeder.

The flicker of a pigeon flock doing their town circuit.

I've spotted four toads! Two mating, the small male clinging onto the fat back of the bigger female. The other two are in the compost bag under the garden seat. I do love toads. They've found our little pond, so we'll always have them now.

Brett and I are birding at Hayle. I do love being with him. He seems to understand things without me telling him, and he likes me no matter how geeky I look. He's never mentioned my bad skin or anything. He seems to like me the way I am. I've come with him and his Dad to a RSPB hide by the lake. I feel like I belong to this group of birders now. My binoculars aren't as powerful as many of the others, but Alistair's here and he has a telescope on a tripod and he gets me to look through it when he finds something of interest. Many birds have been swept off course by the gales and ended up here for a rest. I'm still useless at recognising different species, but Brett is on hand with identification books. We sit on a bank and share our sandwiches. He has Vegemite. It tastes a bit like Marmite, but it's not as strong. I have crunchy peanut butter and banana.

'Have you told Gussie our news?' asks Brett's dad, Steve.

'What news?' I say. I look at Brett and he looks embarrassed.

'We're going home,' he says quietly.

'Oh, okay, ready when you are.'

'No, we're going back to Australia. Newcastle. Home.'

'For a holiday?'

'No. For ever.'

'Oh! But… I thought you liked it here.'

'It's Mum. She misses her family. My gran is getting old and she wants to be with her.'

'Couldn't she come to England?'

'Mum wants to go home. She's not settled here. No job and the climate doesn't suit her. Too wet. Misses the gums,' says Steve. He's not too happy, either.

'Gums?'

'The gum trees. Eucalypts.'

'Oh… When are you leaving?' I ask a glum-looking Brett.

'End of summer term.'

'Do you want to go?'

'No, S'orright here. I like it.' He turns to me and whispers, 'I'm sorry, Guss.'

I can't say anything. I feel as if my new heart has suddenly got heavy and is weighing me down. Why, when I'm so happy, does Brett have to leave?

It's not fair. It's *Not Fair*!

I pretend to look through my binoculars but everything is a blur.

CHAPTER TEN

IN THE PRIVACY of my room I've been crying for quite a while, and my face is puffy and red. I'm a complete mess. I feel betrayed. Why didn't Brett tell me he was leaving? He must have known when we went birding on the Island. He's my only real friend and I think I love him. I don't think I can bear it if he goes away. Australia is too far.

My cats know I'm upset. I sit and look out the window. Bubba is playing with a toy mouse. She's too young to tune in to my emotions. Charlie sits close to me. Flo watches the kitten and is desperate to join the fun but her pride stops her. Rambo lies nearby, looking proud, as if he is the kitten's father.

I knew it couldn't last – this happiness. It never does. Something awful always happens to spoil things.

I have only four months left with Brett.

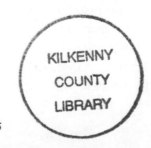

CHAPTER ELEVEN

APRIL 1ST – MUM'S BIRTHDAY. She's ancient.

I have made a cake and it's hidden in Mrs Thomas's fridge. It's traditional for me to play a trick on Mum before she gets her real present. This year, I decided not to be so childish. I know she's never taken in by my tricks anyway; she goes along with them to humour me.

Still no letter from the donor family.

We're eating out – Mum, Alistair and me. Lunch at a beach café. I would normally choose mussels and chips but I'm not allowed shellfish any more, not since the transplant – can't risk food poisoning. So I have pizza with cheese and anchovies. I never used to like anchovies but for some strange reason I do now. Perhaps my donor was Italian? Blue cheese and unpasteurised cheeses are a no-no, too.

It's cloudy and showery, so we run back home – yes, I can run – it's extraordinary to be able to do that again. When I fetch the cake and present it to Mum she's delighted – until she sees that instead of writing '53' in icing, I've put '63'!

For one moment Alistair thinks it's true and he looks at her in horror. It would make her eighteen years older than him. Then he realises the joke and remembers the day.

After Mum has chased me round the kitchen table several

times armed with a wooden spoon, we eat it (the cake, not the wooden spoon). It's not bad for a beginner. Sponge cake with strawberry jam in the middle.

Mrs Thomas gives Mum a brooch, which was her mother's. She has no children of her own and she says she would like her to have it. It's very pretty – a blue enamel and silver bird.

Alistair has given her another necklace. He gave her amber for Christmas. This time, it's turquoise. It's very lovely. I also gave her a book – Rumer Godden's *The River*, which I'm sure she'll love. A car-boot bargain. The recipe book is a great success.

I'm collecting old postcard messages. It's Mum's fault. She started me on it. Car-boot sales and flea markets are ideal hunting grounds. Old postcards cost hardly anything. First I only looked at cards from St Ives, but some are quite expensive. Then I discovered that the messages were more fascinating than the images usually, and it's a bit like snooping or being a voyeur, so it feels rather naughty. Except that postmen can read them, so they aren't really private messages. So now I look at the cheap postcards but turn them over so I can read what's on the reverse. On the back of an undated picture postcard of 'St Ives, Old Houses':

> *To Mr Jack Rogers, Tuckingmill, Camborne.*
> *Remember me when*
> *This you see, though*
> *Many miles apart.*
> *If others have my*
> *Company, 'tis you*
> *That have my heart.*
> *Though separation*

Be our lot, Darling
I'll forget you not.
Flo

To accompany a 'Comic Card': *Tramp – Yus mum, I've seen better times. I used to be an* ORGANIST. *Lady – What made you give it up? Tramp – Me monkey died.*

The message:

Can you sing for me
At the Baptist Chapel?
We are willing to pay
£2–2–0 for your services.
WI Millington

Another, Padstow, July 1907:

Dear Arthur,
This is a dangerous place.
Many ships have been wrecked here.
I wish you and All were here too.
C Bradley

More postcard messages. Cadgwith, 1905:

Dear Nell,
Mother has just returned from seeing
your mother. She is splendid. Willie
is managing fine. I suppose you have
not heard of the death of poor Mrs James
(Syd's mother).
She died in a fit yesterday,

Yours to a cinder,
Bert

Another postcard message (not a Cornish card though,
but I have kept it anyway). Porthcawl, Glamorgan, 1947:

My dear Eileen,
Arrived OK. *The rabbits welcomed me as a*
long-lost brother! The fish here are the most
modest I have yet met, (no cod!) The country is
lovely (it beats Kent! Must say that, Fred
is vetting this!) Having a really grand time,
Love, Stan

(Fred is writing separately. He cannot pour out
his soul in so small a space. Letter from him
follows in about two years!)

They are like small poems, these postcard messages. I've
been reading a lot of poetry lately. Poets seem to know what
to say, when I haven't the words for how I feel.

I'm putting the postcards into a large scrapbook. I've
got birthday cards, interesting labels, pictures cut from
magazines, letters I've had, poems I like in there too. Nature
notes, photos I take. It's a visual diary, or a decorative
journal, or a... a scrapbook.

Note: I find a very attractive lump of regurgitated gull food
on the garden table. It's made up of tiny brown crab feet,
and unidentifiable white bits – cartilage, probably of crabs.
I wish I'd kept another lump of gull vomit I found some
time ago. It was made of whole tiny crabs and was like an
intricate piece of porcelain or ivory carving. Maybe I could

suggest it as a new hobby for Gabriel – collecting gull vomit.
He'd like that.

23 April 2000 – Easter Day. At the Darlings. Fay has arrived with chocolate eggs for Gabe and me, Phaedra and Troy. Gabriel is impressed by my gift of gull vomit.

Zennor the puppy is mad. She never walks anywhere, she bounds like a racehorse and she's getting huge. I have to stand out of her way when she heads for me, or she'd knock me over. After lunch Gabriel and I have an Easter egg hunt in the dripping wet garden and it takes forever, but I make sure that Gabriel finds most of them. He knows all the best places to look: in the hen shed, for one, in the rabbit hutch, and under the salad leaves growing in the polytunnel. I found one in his tree basket and one in Treasure's favourite hiding place, and where she had her last litter of kittens – the airing cupboard. It hadn't melted yet. It reminded me of Grandpop hiding his pear drops in the airing cupboard. Mum said it was to protect my teeth from decay. It was a waste of time. I have such a sweet tooth – I can sniff out a jelly baby or a chocolate button at a hundred paces.

Phaedra is out with her biker boyfriend, a musician in a punk rock band, and Troy is surfing, of course. I have only ever met them both for about two hours altogether as they are such busy people.

It's raining, so we don't spend much time in the garden, though I do get the opportunity to climb into Gabriel's tree. PT I no longer suffer from vertigo. He has a whole life in the trees, like the monkeys in the Babar stories. He's clever with his hands, like his father. Leaves are coming out on the tree and the smell of wood is pungently fragrant – resinous. We sit quietly dripping in black plastic ponchos, like two bedraggled crows, side by side.

'Caw, caw,' I crow, pecking at a chocolate egg. Rain drips from the makeshift roof of a sheet of plywood onto our heads. Beneath us the three ducks worry the grass.

'We're getting soaked, Gabe, I'm going inside.'

'Caw, caw!' he says, flapping his shiny black wings, and follows me. He's over his grief for Terry the Terrible, his tarantula. I'm not sure he's forgiven Troy yet for killing it. (I wonder who cleared up the mess?) But he does already have a new enthusiasm: carnivorous plants – like Venus Flytraps and pitcher plants. He keeps them in the polytunnel. They look primeval, or just plain evil. Sticky and smelly. Marvellous. They don't need feeding as they simply wait for any likely victim to land in their sweet stickiness and die slowly.

The family next door are here for the weekend. Through the party wall we hear the girls shouting at each other. Bubba went in their open front door and made friends with them. She's such a tart!

Mum chats to the parents over the fence. I do hope she doesn't invite them for supper. They're too loud and Londony. I've gone off London people. I prefer locals, like Mrs Thomas and Bridget. Except that Bridget is Irish originally.

The holiday goes too quickly. We have some sunny days and Mum comes to Porthmeor once with me for a picnic. The beach family are there and we sit with them, but it gets chilly early in the evening and everyone leaves the beach.

Brett and I manage one day at Hayle estuary, birding. Steve drives us. I want to gather samphire but it's not tall enough yet. We see loads of egrets, dotterel, swans, Brent geese, grey herons and a flock of lapwings. We don't mention Australia.

I'm very excited about going to school for the first time

since we moved here from London. I don't feel anxious, though Mum is. She's worried I won't cope. But I can't wait.

CHAPTER TWELVE

Note: Five swans pass over the house this perfect pink morning, the sea a huge silver platter. The swans' bellies are the colour of flamingos. A wren flickers on the trellis. At the mouth of the harbour there are about ten gulls floating in the water, dipping and bobbing. It's a bathing party. They aren't fishing, they are grooming. It's like the hairdressers – all these women sitting close together, having their hair shampooed and cut.

MY FIRST DAY at school! It was all a bit overwhelming. Too many big people in the corridors, so much noise. I'm not used to it. It was exciting though. I felt almost normal. But now I have a headache.

'How was it, Gussie? Did you have a good time?'

'I have a very nice teacher – Miss Welding. And I saw Brett's dad, but I didn't have Science or Maths today. And I saw Bridget at lunchtime.' What I didn't tell her was that I am in the same class as Bridget's sister, Siobhan. And when Miss Welding realised we knew each other, she put me next to her. What a nightmare! Siobhan sneered at me every time she caught my eye, but I ignored her. She'd be really pretty if she didn't sneer so much.

I am very behind in lots of ways, but I think I can catch up.

Wish I didn't have to see sss (Shit-face Slut Siobhan) every day though.

I saw Brett in the distance but he didn't see me, at least I don't think he did. He was with his mates. I felt guilty. Why? Why do I feel ashamed that I'm unhappy about Brett leaving? It's nothing to be ashamed of, is it? I can't help loving him. He doesn't know that I love him. I don't think he really wants to go back to Australia.

'Homework?'

'No, nothing.'

Still no letter.

I'm watching Flo marching. She's usually cross or in a huff, especially since the kitten arrived on her territory, but when she finds a woolly blanket she goes all daft and soft, marching. Her 'fingers' open on one front paw and the claws extend and grasp the blanket, then she does the same with the other paw. Alternate paws march slowly. Her eyes have glassed over and she's dribbling, hypnotised. She's not embarrassed. Her eyes have narrowed to slits. The blanket has become her mother's stomach and she's back in her kitten-hood, drinking her mother's milk.

'Mum, did you breastfeed me?'

'I've told you before, Gussie, no. You were fed by tube for weeks. You were too weak to suck. But I expressed breast milk for you.'

'Did you know about Brett and his family going back to Australia?' I choke out the words. Saying them makes them real.

'Yes, Gussie, I did know.'

I say nothing. I get up and walk away. Charlie follows me upstairs.

Mum knocks on my door. 'Can I come in?'

'Yes.'

She holds me close and I smell her warm body smell, the faintly oniony breath, and a minty mouthwash, Mum smell. A safe smell. A smell that makes me feel small and protected, but angry, and confused.

'Why didn't you tell me?'

'Because I thought he ought to tell you himself.'

My tears wet her shoulder; snot dribbles onto her sweatshirt. She brushes back a stray hair from my eyes.

'Your hair needs a trim. So does mine. Mrs Lorn is coming tomorrow. Spring-cleaning.'

'I hope you don't intend to let her cut our hair.'

I giggle at my own joke and she laughs.

'Come on sweetie-pie, blow your nose and help me with supper. French onion soup with loads of Gruyère.'

'I suppose you want me to grate the cheese?'

'Good for your pectorals.'

Charlie leaps down from the desk and follows us downstairs. Flo has settled on a blanket at the end of my bed and looks crossly at me. Bubba is under the bed with Rambo. I hope Rambo doesn't turn her into an agoraphobic like him.

Alistair has set up my computer. It's brill!

I'm teaching myself to type. I've got a book that tells you how to do it in a week. I'm on day three. It's an entirely other language. We have them at school, computers, not books (we do have books, but not as many as I thought there would be) so I'll soon pick it up.

There's a cold strong wind and all over town; gulls huddle on rooftops, heads to the wind. At dusk I'm surrounded by gulls. Soaring, gossiping, weaving, they are sky-dancing. Hundreds, maybe thousands, inhabiting the air, gathering before the dark, they gradually disperse until only one or two cross the sky, high, alone. Where have they all gone? They have left roof, chimneys, church tower, to go to the cliff ledges, close to the sound of the sea. The church clock sounds six. There's a grey ship halfway between the pier and the far coast of Gwithian. A jackdaw sits on the orange ridge tiles of the house in front above a dribbled stream of gull shit on the slate roof.

The last gulls move away from the town, like people on a moving stairway, up and away, following each other on the same trail. And later, at eleven, I hear them, a rising tumult, a choir in chorus, communicating in the fog and gloom, the thick black air.

Last night there was a storm and the town gulls are nowhere to be seen. Two tankers sit out the storm in the bay, bows plunging and rising sickeningly. Roof tiles quiver and lift and every window and door rattles. I'm writing a poem about it:

> *Not one gull rides the windy sky,*
> *roofs are silent and grey.*
> *blackbirds own the town today.*
>
> *One jackdaw braves the violent air,*
> *waves breach Smeaton's Pier,*
> *two ships hunker in the bay.*
>
> *Palm heads are raving Rastafarians,*
> *squalls squabble with waves*
> *and the grey sky is full of spray.*

It's not finished yet. I need to work on it. But writing on the computer is so easy – I can move words and lines and verses and place them somewhere else: cutting and pasting.

I'm doing gym at school. My muscles are still weak, but I'm improving. Being little helps with gymnastics. Not so much bulk to shift and lift. It reminds me of a wooden toy my grandpop made when I was little. It's a trapeze artist who looks like Rita Hayworth, who he obviously had a thing about. She has a red bikini and black curly hair, red lips and heavy eye make-up. She hangs on twisted strings between two wood poles and when you press the poles together she leaps up onto the top string and somersaults, or balances on the top before falling elegantly over. I still have it. He was good at making things. Sailors have to be self-sufficient – do their own sewing and mending etc. *I* used to be good at climbing and balancing when I was little, before my heart slowed me down.

I can't use the swimming pool for a year PT – there's risk of infection. But I am attending an after-school first-aid course. I need to make up for lost time and learn everything I can whenever I get the opportunity. Having watched my transplant nurses and doctors I feel that it would be a good idea to be able to resuscitate someone who has collapsed. It must be amazing to bring someone back from death. I wonder if Alistair has ever had to do that? We practice on an armless, legless plastic patient called George. We give him the kiss of life. It's fun. Weird, but fun. A new poem:

The Kiss of Life

George lets me put my warm lips to his,
breathe into his cold mouth.
I press down on his naked chest

but he cannot hold me close.
My plastic love has no arms or legs,
but I'll give him the hint of life,
he'll give me a hint of love.

I don't like it yet, but I'll work on it. Could turn it into a comic poem – armless rhyming with harmless?

Brett is doing the first-aid course too. I had no idea when I signed up for it. Honest. He's still acting strangely towards me though, as if he feels guilty that he is going back to Australia. Which is silly. Children are totally at the mercy of their parents' decisions. We have no say in where we live. Perhaps his parents will get killed in an accident and he'll be an orphan and Mum could adopt him, then he could live with us. No, that's a terrible thing to think. Perhaps he could say he doesn't want to go back to Australia and Hayley and Steve could say that he can only stay if we have him to live with us. Or perhaps he could become really ill the day before they leave England and he comes to stay with us and I nurse him back to health, he falls in love with me and swears he'll never leave.

I am sitting in my window seat, Bubba purring on my lap. Charlie is looking with hatred and jealousy at her, her eyes narrowed to slits of venom. I reach over and stroke her, but she goes off in a huff. Oh dear, it's difficult keeping them all happy. Bubba has settled in beautifully. Flo hasn't eaten her – I think she would have done by now if she was going to. Rambo adores her. It's only Charlie who has had her nose put out of joint – what a funny expression. Mum found a book on sayings and expressions at a car-boot sale.

Can't wait to go to the next one. I have pocket money to spend on postcards and second-hand books.

CHAPTER THIRTEEN

'Here's another nice mess you've gotten me into.'
Oliver Hardy, *The Sons of the Desert,* 1933

MY PROBLEMS:

1. I feel guilty about surviving when my donor had to die.
   I know it's not my fault, but I can't help it. Maybe if
   I knew more about how my donor died, who it was, I
   might feel better. Had she been ill for a long time? Was
   she in a traffic accident? Did she donate her own organs
   or did her next of kin make the decision to give someone
   else a chance of life? Wish they'd write to me.
2. I am miserable about Daddy not being part of my family
   any more. He and Mummy just can't live together. Apart
   they can be friends. I do want them both to be happy,
   but that means I have to live without him. (I suppose
   I could live with him some of the time, but not at the
   moment. Can't see him dealing with my problems and
   healthcare, not like Mum does. Anyway he has a full-
   time job, whereas Mum has chosen to stay at home to
   look after me.
3. I miss my grandpop and grandma. I am no longer stunned
   by grief, but there's a large hole in my life where they
   were. I miss their hugs, their age. By that I mean their
   wisdom, I suppose. They were old so had accumulated

lots of knowledge and common sense. But I have now got a new family – the Darlings, Daddy's Cornish family. I do like all of them, though I don't really know Troy and Phaedra yet. They are busy with surfing – both of them; and drumming – Phaedra. They are both much older than me. Gabriel is a sweetheart, but much younger than me.

4. I'm anxious about my new organs. Having had acute rejection, I know how easy it is to become dangerously ill. (It has made me more careful about looking after myself. If I hear someone cough or sneeze or even sniff I stay away from them. I can't afford to catch a cold in case it becomes a chest infection. I have to take my medications and do my health checks each day. It's become part of life, like washing. I'm lucky. I still have my arms and legs, my sight, hearing, my brain – I AM A BEAR OF VERY LITTLE BRAIN – as Pooh says. But I am hoping to enlarge my brainpower at school.)

5. Precious – he didn't survive. And I thought he was so strong. And he liked me. I wish I had known him better. I wish I had kissed him, told him how much I liked him, while I could.

6. Most of all, I'm unhappy that Brett will be leaving forever. I have only just started to get to know him and he's going. I can't bear it. My first love, and it's over before it's begun.

7. School – I don't know if I really like it. It's not as good as I thought it would be. It's rather disappointing to meet an English teacher who hasn't read the books I've read. Hasn't even heard of Mary Webb or Carson McCullers. But on the other hand the school library is full of stuff I've never heard of. Lots of paperbacks with pink covers – aimed at young girls. Me, I suppose. Can't wait to read

them. It will be an education.

8. sss. Mum says stay away from her. How can I when I am sat next to her at school? How can she be so horrid when her little sister is so endearing? Even in her school uniform Siobhan manages to look like a slut. All the boys in class like her of course. Because she's got breasts. You can see their eyes drawn like magnets to those bumps. I want bumps too. I have put on weight since the transplant but not in the right places. Mum says I will develop soon enough. I'm still about the same size as a ten-year-old, rather than a twelve-year-old. My new heart and lungs and circulation are working well. That's the main thing. And she's right. I do feel amazingly energetic and the sensation of breathing deeply is miraculous. I can run! Run!

9. I promised Grandpop that I would make something beautiful and extraordinary. But what? What am I good at?

My great-grandfather's photographs and a few of mine are being hung at the London Film Archive in the autumn, though I haven't heard anything from Daddy about it recently. But he promised... but I don't suppose my pictures are really good – it's just that I am a master's great-granddaughter and it will make a good subject for an exhibition. Perhaps they'll call it 'First and Last Images' or 'Keeping it in the Family'.

I haven't shown my poems to anyone yet, and I don't really know my new English teacher well enough to show her.

Perhaps I could ask Brett's mum. Hayley's a good teacher, and I wish I still had her home tutoring me. She loves poetry and fiction and has read the authors I love best – like Jane Austen and George Eliot.

Amazing news! Alistair is the new owner of Peregrine Cottage, the place we rented before Mum found our house in town. He's inherited it from his father. He's taking us there at the weekend.

I have mixed feelings about the house. When we stayed there I was too ill to enjoy it and I was lonely and unhappy, having just lost Grandpop and Grandma and having left Daddy behind in London, and my friends. It's on the edge of a steep cliff and it is difficult to get to. You have to walk down a rough path, cross the branch-line railway track, take the coast path and walk down steps. Quite a hike. Getting back up to the road is exhausting – or it was for me. But once you are at the cottage it's lovely, unique, overlooking the curve of a high sea cliff and a white beach that stretches away to an estuary and sand dunes.

And it's there that I met Brett: on the coast path. He saved my camera from certain death when I dropped it over the cliff. We clicked straight away, over binoculars. The peregrine of Peregrine Cottage. That's what we saw together. Our first bird. I must stop thinking about Brett. It hurts as if there's a sharp stone in my throat – as if he's died. And he'll still be in the world. Not my part of the world, but the opposite side of it.

We park at the top of the hill and walk down to the house. There's a stiff wind but the sun is shining. The huge beach is empty as usual apart from the birds – oystercatchers paddling busily at the edge of the sea and last year's young gulls still mottled brown like tabbies. They are sitting facing the wind, listening to the wise words of an adult gull. Or that's what it looks like.

The thing is, I feel so full of energy that the place has changed for me. It's as if my eyes are new, not just my heart and lungs. I don't look at the steep cliff with fear and loathing any more; I am not dizzy at the height, and I am not breathless.

'I'm going to the beach.'

'Come inside first,' says Mum.

The door creaks open and I smell something familiar… oh yes, the musty smell of old books. They are still here, lining the wooden walls.

'Was he a writer? Your father? I always thought he must be.'

'No, a GP, like me. He was in a home for the last few years though. Alzheimer's.'

'What happened to your mother?'

'Died in childbirth when my sister was born. She died too. I was seven.'

'How sad! Did he never remarry?'

'No. Terrified of women. Wouldn't have them in the house.'

'Except for your mother and Mrs Lorn,' I say.

'Except for my mother and Mrs Lorn.'

'Look – Fabre's *Insects*!' I am delighted that all the old books I read and enjoyed are still here. It seems ages ago that we rented the cottage, but it was only last year.

'Take it Gussie, take any book you like.' Alistair throws open the windows. The tall trees whisper and the bamboos swish and bend.

'Do you remember your twelfth birthday? The total eclipse?' Mum holds me close suddenly.

'It was foggy and dark, but then at the moment of the total eclipse all the cameras flashed and it was as if the stars had fallen and were twinkling all around us on every beach.'

'I was at Marazion. The sun was shining there. It was ideal,' says Alistair.

I explore the little house, sniffing at the books, seeing the old pictures and my old metal bed.

'Are you going to live here now?' I ask Alistair.

'Yeah, why not? I could rent or sell my flat and move out here. Great for birding.'

'Can we come for a weekend?'

'Gussie!'

'I know – may we and please!'

'Yes, Gussie, if you want to.' I look at Mum and she nods.

'Give Alistair a chance to move in first, Gussie.'

'Do you remember when we gathered mussels, Mum?'

'Tide's out, we could get some today,' says Alistair.

An hour later we have enough mussels for supper. My fingers are sore from picking them. I sit on a rock and gaze at the waves. From beach level they are huge, but broken up, so there are no surfers here today. Gannets plunge into the sea off the point. There must be a shoal of fish.

It's hypnotic, watching the sea. It's never blue all over. The deep water is grape-purple and closer in it's a glaucous green, like cooked cabbage. The sea is busy crashing onto the rocks below me, sucking back and exposing black shiny clumps of mussels and red weed. Always coming and going, relentless and huge. Is that why people come to the seaside – to watch something that will never end?

'What was he like, your father?'

'Funny old chap. Eccentric. Amateur entomologist. Read a lot.'

'Obviously!' I say, delighted that all these books are mine to read again. I wish I had known his father though. I think we might have had a few things in common.

'What was his name?'

'Peregrine Holman Dobbs.'

'Seriously?'

'Yep.'

'But... so Peregrine Point was named after him?'

'No. The falcons that habitually nest close by gave the place its name. Some sort of fly was his area of special interest, I think.'

'Fly? Like Fabre's *Life of the Fly*? There's a hardback copy here.'

'Yes, though Dad never got round to producing a book on the subject.'

I eventually find the book. It has a linen cover of dark green and the rough-edged, hand-cut pages are browned on the edges and unevenly sewn in. There are no illustrations. I might get around to reading it one day. But there are so many books I want to read first.

'We had a practically tame gull when we stayed here,' Mum is telling Alistair. 'I was convinced it was the spirit of my sailor father. We called him Pop and he came into the house and helped himself to cat food.'

'Really?' Alistair looks taken aback, as if he thinks maybe Mum is out of her mind, and maybe he shouldn't have committed himself to loving her after all.

'Yes, and Gussie got on the roof to save his life. He had swallowed a fishing hook and line and the line got caught on the ridge tiles. It was horrible.'

'Gussie climbed onto the roof?'

'She was very brave. Had vertigo too, at the time.'

'What happened?'

I remember the feel of the gentle beak in the palm of my hand. 'Pop freed himself and flew off, and came back for a couple of days, took food from my hand. But then he disappeared.'

'And that was when Gussie developed a chest infection.'

'Yes, I remember,' says Alistair. They look lovingly at each other.

We explore the garden – it's more of a jungle than it was before. The herbs that Mum planted have been overgrown by bamboos. In fact, bamboos have colonised most of the garden, but there are tree ferns and palms, tall and exotic. In some parts you can't see the sea, only hear it, the waves sucking at the cliff below. Alistair says he must get a gardener.

'What happened to the old one?'

'Met a rich woman and married her, and she whisked him away to her pad in Florida.'

'Seriously?'

He raises his expressive eyebrows at me and smiles.

Back home we scrape barnacles from the shells and pull out the byssus – that's the name of the stringy threads that anchor them to a rock. The phone rings. Mum picks it up, giggles, says 'No, thank you, I don't need one – yet,' and puts it down.

'I don't know,' she says. 'Now I'm over fifty the only obscene phone calls I get are for stair lifts or double glazing.'

Poor Mum, growing old. It's wonderful to be young and to suddenly have my life given back to me – ten, twenty years, with luck. Maybe more, who knows? A lifetime. Whatever I do I mustn't squander it. In Zimbabwe the life expectancy is only about thirty-five years. And that's for healthy people. Or for healthy people and the seriously sick – like people with AIDS. But people there with any congenital disease, like mine, or cystic fibrosis, have no chance at all. So I have been given a gift, simply because I have accidentally been born in England. I have the opportunity of doing something with my life. I have not been discarded. I have the unique chance of living a life that means something. But what?

I'm not allowed moules. *Quel dommage!* I get to have lots of frites though. And salad: roasted beetroot with balsamic vinegar, tiny tomatoes, pepper, basil and oregano. Mmm! And a glass of elderflower juice.

'I hated beetroot as a child,' says Mum. 'My mother mixed it in with lettuce leaves, hard-boiled eggs and tomatoes. It stained everything purple.'

'This is yummy,' I say, and she smiles smugly.

I keep thinking about Presh. His short life. The time I knew him. We were in the weird World of the Sick; we would never have met if we hadn't both had transplants. What might have happened if he had lived? I would have got to know him more, liked him even more. I did like him so much. As much as I like Brett. I'm confused. I think I love Brett. I feel sick thinking about him going away for ever. But I felt the same way about Precious. He was so... beautiful and... gentle... and exciting and foreign, different. I wish I'd kissed him. Should I kiss Brett before he goes back to Australia? Or are we just birding friends? I know he likes me, he said so. He prefers me to sss even though she's pretty. Does he expect me to kiss him? I don't feel ready to kiss any boy except as a friend.

'Mum, how old were you when you first kissed a boy?'

'Fifteen... he had red hair, great legs. Tennis player. He was seventeen. I used to cycle past the tennis club ten times a day so I could see him in his shorts.'

'When did you kiss him?'

'My first dance, the last waltz. I wore silver sandals and a turquoise dress. I had to stand on tiptoe and he bent down to kiss me. Howard. He was called Howard Leggett. Became a dentist. Think – if I'd married him I'd be Lara Leggett.'

'Did you ever kiss him again?'

'No, never. It was a one-off. I couldn't breathe and hated it. I went off the idea for a couple of years. I'm still a lousy kisser.' She gives me a hug. 'Who were you thinking of kissing?'

'No one in particular. It was a general enquiry.'

At school on my second day, we had a talk on sex and health, with a disgusting video all about sexually transmitted diseases. Yuk! How anyone ever has sex is beyond me. You can get cervical cancer, herpes, chlamydia, all sorts of horrible things that ruin your life, not to mention pregnancy. It's put me off completely. I think kissing's safe though.

I've been thinking. Both the boys I have liked have been foreign – Australian Brett and Zimbabwean Presh. Perhaps I'll always be attracted to boys who aren't English.

'How many boyfriends did you have before you married Daddy?'

'Don't remember – dozens, I think. You forget, I was old when I got married.'

'Did you ever love anyone else before Daddy?'

'Gussie, I'm trying to draw. I can't concentrate with you asking me questions.'

'No, but did you?'

'Shoo, make me a cup of tea and I'll tell you.'

I make us both tea. It's raining and the cats want me to sit on the sofa and cuddle.

Mum comes down from her 'studio' and sits with me.

'I did have a man I loved before Daddy. But he was married, so...'

'What? Married? You didn't try to steal him from another woman, did you?'

'Certainly not. I loved him hopelessly for ten years, without seeing him.'

'Did he love you?'

'He said he did, but I only really knew him for three weeks. Then he went to New Zealand.'

'Did you ever see him again?'

'Yes, he came to London and got in touch. Said he was getting a divorce. He still thought of me and wanted to know how I felt about him.'

'How romantic!'

'Not really. He'd put on loads of weight and I didn't recognise him. He'd been slim and gorgeous when I knew him. Anyway, I'd met Daddy then.'

Poor Mummy. Ten years of wasted love.

'Are you still sad about Brett leaving?'

'Yes.'

'Darling, there'll be loads of other boys. You'll meet so many.'

'He's not just any boy. He's my best friend.' She doesn't understand. *'What we have here is a failure to communicate.'* *Cool Hand Luke*, Paul Newman, 1967.

After supper – vegetable soup and garlic bread – we watch *Brideshead Revisited*. It's terribly good. I must read the book. So many times the book is better than the movie. I don't know why that should be. Maybe our minds fill in the visuals in a book, and the movie can never live up to our imagination. Or the film actors aren't as we thought the characters look. But *The Last Tycoon* is a great movie and is as good as the book, mainly because it keeps to the words in the book. Robert De Niro makes a perfect Monroe Stahr – aloof, lonely, ruthless and vulnerable all at once. What a great actor!

CHAPTER FOURTEEN

MUM HAS WRITTEN to Agnes at the last address she gave us but hasn't heard back. I wonder what's happened with her. Have her daughters come to England? Is her husband safe? BBC journalists have been banned from reporting from Zimbabwe, so it's difficult getting news. He's possibly in prison.

I have to go to London soon for a routine biopsy and check-up. I'll see Daddy again as we'll be staying at his place for a couple of nights. Mum and he seem to be getting on better since my transplant. At least they're polite to each other over the phone. My illness is what originally split them, and my transplant brought them to some sort of Peaceful Settlement. Or that's how Mum explained it to me. (I think she is nicer to him because now she's got Alistair, and she's happier than when she was alone. Well, she had me, but it's not the same.) And what about Daddy – who has he got to comfort him? He can't seriously love the Snow Queen, can he? There must be the right woman who's not a freak out there somewhere.

Note: Discovered a young gull wandering down the back lane, one wing drooping.

'Mu-um. There's an injured gull.'

'Oh, bloody hell. I'm busy.'
'But we can't ignore it.'
'Don't shout at me.'
'So, what if it dies on our step and we haven't helped?'
'I'm busy!'
I say nothing.
'Oh, Gordon Bennett!'
She puts down her drawing and comes to look. I'm right.
It's not right. Broken wing or something.
'Find a cat basket.'

I have always wanted to come here – to the Mousehole Bird
Hospital. It's much smarter than I imagined from the book
I read about the sisters who started it. They had a foreign
name, Inglesias or something. They began by looking after
any injured bird, and they discouraged the local boys from
hurting the gulls. It was a favourite Mousehole pastime
– stoning baby gulls! They offered money to any boy who
saved a bird. And it worked – bribery usually does, with me
anyway. What if the boys stoned the birds, then rescued them
and took them to the hospital to get the money? Anyway the
bird hospital just built up naturally.

We give the young gull to the woman in charge and she
examines it. No broken wing, but she says they'll keep it
there and feed it until it's strong enough to fly, then they'll
release it. The drooping wing was probably an indication
that it was in distress. Even if the parents feed a fallen young
gull, they hardly ever survive long enough to fly. Ideally they
need to be off the ground when they take their first flight. In
the wire enclosures are pigeons and crows mostly and a few
gulls, looking rather sad and quiet. They've got trees and
things to hop on and lovely views over the sea. I expect they
feel homesick.

When we get home Bubba and Rambo are hanging out in Mrs Thomas's garden. Rambo sits majestically on a bench and Bubba's underneath playing with his tail. They ignore me.

The phone rings and Mum answers it. She giggles and says 'I'm not telling you.' Then, 'Yes, it was, actually,' and laughs out loud.

'Was that another rude phone call?' I ask.

'You could say that. Alistair wanted to know the colour of my poo!'

'Why?'

'His is dark red and he was worried he'd got cancer. It's the beetroot, of course.'

'Oh, mine's red too. I thought it was the drugs.' How odd to think of a doctor worrying about having cancer, but I suppose they get ill too.

I'm having an interesting time with my computer. A tiny spider has disappeared into one of the portholes, or whatever they're called. It must seem like a tunnel into a deep cavern, hanging with metal stalagmites/tites? Is it tites that go up and mites that go down or the other way around? It hasn't reappeared. What it is doing in there? Is it rearranging my files, building its own website? www.eensyweensyspider. com? Was it pregnant? Will there be thousands of tiny spiders living in my computer? Does it matter?

I've decided to go to Porthmeor Beach this evening after school. Mum won't come. She's cooking for Alistair. Fried haloumi cheese on a bed of salad leaves, hard-boiled eggs and herbs, fried new potatoes with spring onions and anchovies, tiny tomatoes with basil and parsley, and tinned tuna. It was my idea, the tuna. I prefer it to fresh tuna. I'm meeting Bridget there, and Claire is coming with Gabriel – for a picnic. I think

Mum is pleased to have some time alone with Alistair. And I'm pleased to have some time away from them.

There's a large group of people from school. I recognise a few, including sss. Bridget and I are sitting several metres away from them, on our own, against the studio wall, near the beach house where the girl with the hairless cat lives. Their ladder is there, leading from their door to the beach, and there's a blanket on the beach, with a blue and white beach umbrella, but they aren't there at the moment.

Bridget has brought sandwiches and fruit, and so have I. She has a wetsuit and wants to go in the sea. I haven't got a wetsuit and the water is freezing. I leap about and watch her on her belly board. It does look fun. She lets me have a go. The water is icy, but so clear and clean. I love it. The group from school are surfing, or some of them are, including sss.

'My sister's an awful show-off,' says Bridget.

'She's quite a good surfer though, isn't she?' I say reluctantly.

'She's only doing it to impress Joe.'

'Who's Joe?'

'He's the boy with red hair.'

Joe is obviously the main man, the champ. He uses his board as if it's part of his body, swerving and yawing into the waves. I know nothing about it but he looks good. Easy Rider of the waves.

I suddenly notice two boys of about 16 sitting on their own further down the beach. They are concentrating hard on something. A gull gets close to them, takes a piece of bread from the sand and flies off, dragging a plastic bottle on a string snare around its leg. They laugh. I am so shocked I do nothing. They're making another, laying a loop of string on the sand, covering it, placing a piece of bread in the middle and waiting to entice another poor bird to take the bait.

Without thinking, I run to them and sweep up two handfuls of sand and scoop it into their faces. The bigger one goes to throw some back at me but only threatens. They both have sand in their hair and eyes.

'You cowardly bullies! That bird will die because of what you've done. I've phoned the RSPCA. They're on their way.' I lie. They look disbelieving, but they are embarrassed, I can tell, to be shouted at by a puny twelve-year-old on a public beach, surrounded by people. I don't wait to hear what they have to say. I am shaking with fury. As I get back to our beach towels Bridget says, 'What did you say to them? They're leaving.'

How can people be so cruel? The bird will die a slow death, unable to swim and feed and fly, dragged down as if it had a ball and chain around its ankle. I find I am crying with frustration and anger and sadness. It reminds me of what WH Hudson wrote about local youths torturing and killing birds, and the Mousehole sisters having to bribe the local boys so they would stop harming the birds. And I wonder if anything will ever change human nature. Will there always be cruelty?

'You're so brave, Gussie, I wouldn't dare do that.'

It's lucky we're near a crowd or they might have attacked me. I didn't think.

'Guss, what happened?'

'Brett! Oh Brett, did you see what those boys did?'

'No, just arrived. Heard someone say you threw sand at a couple of blokes. How come?'

Bridget gives him an exaggerated account of the incident, making much of my instinctive reaction. He's impressed.

'Do you mind Bridget? I want to go home,' I say.

'S'okay, Gussie, I can go later. Mum doesn't mind.'

'You sure?'

'I'll walk you home, Guss,' Brett offers. 'You look crook.'

It's upset me, losing my temper. I'm still trembling. As we walk along the beach to the steps, sss looks sideways at us and smirks and says something I can't hear to Leah, who is also in my class. I keep looking forward but trip over my own feet and lurch forwards. Derisive laughter from the beach group. Brett grabs my arm and stops me from falling. He hangs onto my hand and we walk together along the beach, all those eyes following us. I feel suddenly free of anger and frustration and happy to be alive. If he is only here for a short time before he goes back to Australia, I'll make the most of it. His hand is cool and hard, and holds mine firmly as we stride up Porthmeor Hill.

'Where's your bike?' I ask.

'I left it by the beach. I'll collect it later, no worries.'

That means he left the bike so he could hold my hand. How romantic is that!

'I can't believe you're going back to Australia.'

'Nah, me neither. I have good mates and I like it here.'

'Yeah.'

We walk in silence, only the laughing, uncaring gulls above us. The clock on the church tower strikes the hour. Large grey clouds bulge from the west, sweeping low over the town and bay. Somewhere an ambulance siren wails.

'Would you like to come in for tea?'

'Nàh, no worries. I better get my bike and get home, thanks.'

It's changed from a warm spring day to a wintry dusk. A flock of pigeons circle the town, while gulls gather and clamour, encouraging each other to go home to the cliffs before night falls. I suppose that's where they go, though when we were out at the cliff house, many second year juvenile gulls gathered on the big beach at dusk, sitting or standing on the dry sand near the cliffs, talking and preening, or sleeping with heads twisted and tucked under back feathers.

House lights are coming on. A bus turns in to the Malakoff. The sea is flat and green-grey, like unpolished silver.

Charlie sits on the window ledge and gets cross with the roof gulls, who veer away, flustered, as they walk past.

The anchored boats slide slowly on gentle waves.

On the opposite hill, above the terrace of white coastguard cottages, trees are a dark fuzz on the horizon. Someone has poisoned the grass on the slope in front of the cottages. He does it every year, Mrs Thomas says. I think it is a 'he'. Why do it? Mum says it's mean-minded, destroying the plants, insects, leaving a scar on the wooded slopes of Porthminster. Nothing for creatures to feed on. A lifeless slope.

As dusk deepens, rain clouds thicken and cloak the estuary. There are warnings of gales on the weather forecast, though all is calm for now. Yellow car-lights prick the dark streets, become red as they drive away. Plastic windows lose their blindness and become one with the old wood-framed sashes in the gloom. Porthminster point is a black sheep's muzzle lapping the sea. A sudden flurry of gulls, like snowflakes drifting over the roofs.

Mum resuscitates last night's veg soup – puts a heel of parmesan cheese to melt in it and adds tinned cannellini beans and tomato paste.

From my attic window I can see that on the other side of the valley someone still has Christmas lights on a tree in their front garden. They are the sort that flicker off and on; tiny white lights, that look like fireflies. I remember fireflies in Africa, showing us the way home along the beach. Tiny beacons of light hovering before us. As usual with odd animal behaviour – it's a sex thing. The male flashes his light to attract females.

Note: Firefly and Glow-worm. Fireflies are not really flies but of the beetle order Coleoptera. *The males have wings and can fly quite well but the females have shorter wings or are wingless. The flightless females and the larvae are often called glow-worms. Fireflies and glow-worms are capable of emitting light due to a type of chemical reaction called bioluminescence. This process occurs in special light-emitting organs usually in the firefly's lower abdomen. They signal position to each other and flash to attract members of the opposite sex.*

CHAPTER FIFTEEN

Note: Today it's raining hard and cold. Winter has returned and hundreds of gulls and rooks, pigeons and jackdaws are calling and circling the skies over the town. Perhaps they know the world is going to end. Or some calamity has occurred in Birdworld. Oddly, our five roof gulls are looking on, unconcerned from their usual perches on the chimney and dormers. The Easter holiday is nearly over. We've had rain, gales, hot sun, every sort of weather except snow.

NO MAIL. MY cats are in winter mode – sleeping on chests of drawers, on my bed, on the sofa, anywhere high up away from draughts and feet. Always on something soft – a blanket, a discarded jumper, a cushion. Bubba curls up with Rambo; Flo and Charlie sleep alone. Mum is working in her studio, making things. I hear her hammering. I work on a poem about Presh – or Brett, I'm not sure. It's crap and I throw it away. I'm no good at love poems.

'Going out, Mum.'

'In this weather? Wrap up then.'

Bridget and I wander around Woolworths looking at stuff. It's crowded with disgruntled holidaymakers, cross about the rain. We share sweets and she buys a comic.

'Let's go to the library.'

'It's closed.'

'Where else can we go?'

'My house?'

'Is Siobhan there?'

'No. She's surfing.'

'Okay.'

Bridget lives in the estate at the top of the town. She unlocks the door. It's a small modern house with a little front garden and a large back garden. They have distant sea views. She has a black cat called Spike – one of Treasure's kittens. Her mum works as a waitress and her mum's boyfriend is a barman. No one's in. The sitting room is untidy and cold. I have never been here before. It's not as I imagined it would be. There are no books, but loads of videos and celebrity magazines and a huge telly. There's an aquarium with a few blennies and green rocks. It needs cleaning. In fact I think I see one or two dead fish floating on the murky surface.

'Let's play Scrabble,' I suggest, but Bridget doesn't want to. She has a Barbie collection she wants to show me. She's adorable but I wish I had a girl friend my own age.

I need the loo and Bridget says it's at the top of the stairs, but I open the wrong door and while I'm still standing there, taking in the posters of pop star, the discarded clothes on the floor, the stale smell – Siobhan comes up behind me.

'What are you doing in my room? Fuck off, will you!' She pushes me out of the way like some comic-story avenger in her wetsuit, dark hair streaming down her back. Her eyes are full of hate. Scary.

'I was looking for the lavatory. I'm sorry.'

'Lavatory? What's that, posh girl? Why do you use stupid words? You think you're so clever. Get out.' She shuts the door in my face.

CHAPTER SIXTEEN

Note: It would be good to have a little camera attached to one of our roof gulls to follow his journey for a year, see what he sees, experience his flight and feeding. They are scavengers, but in the town they only spend a short time stealing chips or raiding bins. What is their main diet? Fish? Where do they fish? I have seen them sipping the sky of flying insects – mayfly hatchlings, dragonflies, mosquitoes. High in the air with other birds – crows, hawks even. They all enjoy the sudden feast. And we see them on the beach turning over weed and driftwood, presumably finding sand fleas and other insects. They hang around the wake of fishing boats for the throw-away guts, and around rubbish dumps looking for beefburgers, pizzas and other delicacies.

I DON'T FEEL LIKE going to school, for obvious reasons. But I must. We sit not looking at each other, sss and me – the posh girl. I can feel the spite coming off her, like poisoned arrows aimed at me. It's difficult to concentrate on lessons when the person next to you hates you. I've never done anything to her. Why does she dislike me so much? Okay, Brett prefers me to her, and stopped going out with her, but that was her fault. She was two-timing him with his friend Hugo.

At lunchtime I eat my packed lunch at a table as far from sss as I can get. I'm reading *The Great Gatsby*. I can see Brett at a table full of boys, including Liam (Siobhan's brother). It's not as I had hoped – school. I haven't made any new friends. The other girls all have friends already. Anyway, who cares? I'm alive, and that's what matters. I have a lot of things to learn, lots of catching up to do. The bell goes and there's the usual scrum in the corridors to get to the right room. We've got double science – yay!

There's no first-aid course after school. It finished before Easter. There's a chess club but I haven't joined.

I walk home alone.

'What's up, darling? You look glum.'

'Nothing, Mum. I'm okay. Starving. What's for tea? When are we going to London?'

'Day after tomorrow. Train. Daddy's expecting us. He'll be there to see you.'

I feed the cats, though Bubba and Rambo are playing hard to get in Mrs Thomas's garden. She comes out when she hears me calling them.

'I've fed them, my queen. I made them some nice mince, Shandy's favourite, as was.' She picks up Bubba from the top of a plastic water butt and strokes her. A smiling Bubba looks full, her little tummy bulging.

'Oh, okay, thanks.'

Charlie and Flo, after eating, clean themselves thoroughly. I want Charlie on my lap but she pretends she hasn't noticed and flies off in a huff. Flo treats me with her usual contempt and walks off to find a warm spot upstairs.

I turn off the telly and go up to my room, where I do some boring Maths homework. I feel flat, forlorn, forgotten and friendless, fed-up: all the Fs. And no fluffy felines when I need them. '*Fiddle-dee-dee.*' Vivien Leigh as Scarlett O'Hara in *Gone With the Wind*, 1939.

CHAPTER SEVENTEEN

BACK IN LONDON. Daddy is taking us out for supper. He's being very nice to Mummy. She's being civilised to him too. I am nervous about tomorrow – the tests and biopsy. I hate the biopsy. It makes me feel sore afterwards. It will be the first time I've been back to the hospital since Precious died.

'You're quiet, Gussiebun.' Daddy gives me a squeeze.

'How's the Snow Queen? Sorry, Annika?'

'Long gone.'

'Who is it now?'

'No one. Given up women.'

Mum looks as if she doesn't believe him but says nothing.

I'm allowed to choose the restaurant – Italian, round the corner. I have pizza. Afterwards I'm allowed to choose the movie on Dad's home cinema screen. He stays to watch with us. I cuddle up between him and Mum and watch *The Lion King*.

Mimi and Willy from the first floor flat come after dinner and stay for ages. I can't sleep. Too nervous.

There's new post-transplant staff at the clinic. I only recognise one of them – Jason. He does the biopsy and he's very gentle. I hardly feel a thing – just the juddery feeling in my heart when the catheter is inside. There's a tiny cutter that snips a piece of tissue from the new heart muscle. Science-fiction stuff.

I have to do all sorts of exercises – like going on the running machine. The staff are pleased with the results. I'm doing fine.

I still feel f and f,f,f and f.

Note: On the journey back to Cornwall – a field where crows peck and a heron is black against the white sky. The bowed head of a blue-black horse. The swans under the Brunel Bridge hide their heads under their wings.

That's almost like a poem. If I change it a bit...

Plymouth

A bare hill where crows peck
and a heron is black against the white sky.

Under the Brunel Bridge six swans,
heads hidden under wings

and on bright grass, a blue-black horse bows.

CHAPTER EIGHTEEN

Note: A black and white pigeon with striking pattern rules the church tower. An intellectually challenged young gull, still in large season's mottled colours, stooped and bobbing its head, nags its mother for food. A pair of stark-feathered starlings cling to the chimney of the house in front. A duet of gulls – his low call, her higher call, one note at a time. I hear their padding on the flat roof of the dormer. In the gale they hunker down, heads twisted behind them, beaks hidden in the back feathers. Their feathers flutter and bend in the wind. Yellow eyes watch me watching them, suspicious, ready to flee or attack.

HOME AGAIN. THE cats missed me, anyway.

School is the same. sss still sits next to me, casting an evil eye on me. I don't know what's wrong with me. I feel dull and dead inside. Hopeless. The weather echoes my emotions – it's cold for late April, cold enough for snow, with a grey green sky. I can't believe I was sitting on the beach a week or so ago, enjoying the sun.

'Mum, someone at school doesn't like me.'

'Who? Are you sure?'

'It's Siobhan. I have to sit next to her and she hates me.'

'Take no notice, darling, that family has problems.'

'What problems? It doesn't excuse her being horrible to me, does it?'

'She's unhappy, darling, that's why she's being horrid.'

I have a letter!

Dear Gussie,

Thank you very much for the lovely letter that you sent to me. My dear daughter Natalie was a very good person. She wanted to be a nurse and she was working as a nursing assistant with old people. I think you would have liked her. She was nineteen. She had two younger brothers who miss her very much. I am happy that you have survived the operation and that you are well. We had naturally wondered who my daughter's organs had gone to and I am pleased that you have made contact. If you want to know any more, do please write again.

Very best wishes,
Abigail Bridges

Nineteen! So young to have died. Mum and I read it over and over, and we're both tearful. Abigail's given me her address and email so that I can write to her directly.

I've killed six bluebottles tonight since going to bed. I have to get up and stalk them with a fly swat. At first I thought there was one that kept coming back to life – like they do when you don't swat them hard enough. You think they are dead but they revive and live to buzz another day.

It reminds me of a night in France with Mum when we

were sharing a room with a torn mosquito screen on the window. We spent most of the night trying to kill mosquitoes and didn't get any sleep at all.

So why bluebottles at this time of year? Maybe they've hatched on some undiscovered corpse hidden under the bed. Or have they come through the open window to seek warmth? I can usually smell a dead mouse. A smell of gas. The cats never bother with a creature once it's dead. Or only while it's still warm.

In the morning I find Mum cleaning up cat vomit. Copious amounts of it. Green. Flo is the culprit. One interesting bit of vomit contains the innards of a large mouse – liver, heart etc. No wonder she's sick. It looks like she swallowed it whole. There's fur and bones and everything.

I tell Mum about last night's bluebottles and she finds the gall bladder under my bed. Fascinating that cats eat the rest but leave the gall bladder. It must taste really disgusting.

When I die, will it be like going to sleep? Or sinking into a warm sea, fish of every colour and pattern surrounding me, like in Africa? Or will it be like flying? Will I be a bird, like a young gull opening and shutting her wings, jumping up and down on the roof, practising, then one day the air calls to her and she lets the wind lift her up until she is swooping across the harbour, joining all the other white-bellied, grey-winged birds dancing on the wind. Or perhaps I'll be a firefly, my small light flickering on and off, showing someone the way home?

CHAPTER NINETEEN

Note: An orange balloon has just drifted across the sky, over the harbour, and towards the island. A bumblebee is hanging around the cherry tree and a blackbird hops and runs along the trellis.

MUM AND ALISTAIR are doing things to Peregrine Cottage. I hope they don't change it too much. I like it the way it was when we stayed there. Ramshackle. Draughty, Mum calls it. Builders are putting in stairs instead of a ladder and trapdoor, and a new room with a glass roof downstairs. And lots of insulation and a solar panel.

I mooch around the garden. The reeds are about ten metres high and so are the echiums. From their squeaks it sounds as if there are lots of small birds hidden in the foliage. We hung up bird-feeders when we were here and Alistair has filled them with sunflower seeds and peanuts. I think there are blue tit babies in one of the nesting boxes on a tree trunk. When I walk past they go quiet. They make a noise like someone rattling silver foil. The air is warm and humid. I can hear a peregrine call.

'Mum, Alistair! A hawk!' But they don't hear me. I follow the sound with my binoculars and see the bird low over the beach by the cliff. It lands on a rock half-way up, below where it had a nest last year. I wonder if there's a young one there?

'Gussie!' Mum calls from the house.

'Mum I saw the peregrine,' I shout back.

'Come here, we need you.' They want me to choose a colour for the walls of my room.

'My room?'

'Yes, your room, when you come to stay,' says Alistair, showing me the colour charts.

It all comes flooding back – what it's like waking here. Light attacking my eyes as I drift into consciousness. The never-ending thunder and roar of waves on the rocks below making its way into my befuddled brain. Befuddled – I like that word. My dreams floating away before I can grab at them. The cats padding on my bed, telling me it's time for breakfast.

I choose a pale blue-grey, the colour of a gull's wing feathers, for one wall, and white for the rest and the ceiling.

'And I'd like curtains that keep out the morning light, please.'

'Glad you didn't choose pink,' says Alistair.

I've never been a pink person – well, not since I was five. I think little girls have a built in need for pink. It's their favourite colour. I think Mum and Alistair must be getting serious about each other. Will he become my stepfather? I wouldn't be surprised, or sorry. He's a bit of a fuddy-duddy (what a lovely expression!) and an old fogey but he's kind and good for Mum and he listens to me. I supposed he's used to ill people.

'Well I'd like fuschia pink for the main bedroom,' says Mum, sternly. He looks horrified. 'A strong, brave colour.' He is speechless. She bursts out laughing. 'Fooled you!' He hugs her, relieved.

One of his patients had told him that he had gone onto Porthcurno Beach for the first time and there were about thirty dolphins swimming among the surfers, diving and rising among them. He said he would never forget it. I wish I'd been there. Alistair is a very serious person sometimes. I like that. Not like Daddy, who is always flippant, funny, putting on an act. I love my daddy absolutely, no matter what he's like, what he does. He bought me a lovely dressing-gown to take into hospital when I'm an inpatient. But he doesn't realise that they provide all that, specially cleaned so we're not subjected to infection. It's girlie white and pink rose-patterned cotton. I love it. I didn't tell him about the hospital gowns – I didn't want to disappoint him.

At Peregrine Point I go down to the beach on my own and throw a stick for a little terrier who is there with his woman. I've never had a dog. They are much more lively than cats, always wanting to play, but I'd hate to do the poop scoop thing. There's hardly anyone on the beach. A couple of runners on the hard sand, another yappy dog and its man. The oystercatchers are in a group at the water's edge, feeding, and the dog runs towards them barking loudly. No finesse, no stalking, just stupid running and barking. The birds rise derisively just before the dog reaches them, fly a little way up the beach and settle to feed before he gets to them again. It's a pointless game for the dog, and must be irritating the bejebers out of the birds. I remember watching the oystercatchers through binoculars from the cottage – in a group of eight, one was a bully, head down, charging at another who seemed to be excluded from the group. No matter how many times the exile came back and tried to join the group, he was chased away by the bully bird.

What am I to do about sss? It's a horrible feeling when someone doesn't like you. I feel guilty, as if it's my fault. Though I can't see that it is.

CHAPTER TWENTY

Note: There has been heavy rain for two weeks, and two nights after a torrential downpour there were three metres of floodwater in the centre of town. The inshore lifeboat had to rescue people from their flats.

I NOW HAVE MY own email address: gussiestevens@whitebeach. co.uk, and Mrs Bridges has sent me hers.

Dear Mrs Bridges

Thank you very much for replying to my letter. It might seem strange but I feel that your Natalie is with me in everything I do. When I listen to the garden birds' songs, and watch the seagulls fly over the harbour and when I stroke my cats (did she like cats? I do hope so. I have three – Charlie, Flo and Rambo. I did have a kitten called Bubba but she has gone to live with my elderly neighbour). I too like old people very much, and I always have, even before the transplant. I loved my grandparents but they died last year. Maybe I will become a nurse who looks after old people. I would like that. I have wondered how your daughter died. If you don't want to tell me I understand. But because her organs are

*working inside me I would like to know all about
her, including how she lost her life and gave me mine.*
   *By the way, we live in Cornwall. I have a mother
who lives with me, a father who lives in London, and
cousins and a great-aunt who live close by.*

Best wishes, Gussie
PS *The photo is a view from our house of St Ives
harbour.*

We're at the cottage with Alistair, inspecting the damage. The house is fine but about sixty tons of earth have disappeared over the cliff, along with a couple of small elms and several mature hydrangeas, which have ended up at the other end of the beach.

'The engineer says there's no damage to the foundations,' says Alistair. But the landscape of the garden has changed. There is no path along the lower edge, just mud. The cottage, which was always close to the edge, is now even closer.

It was difficult to park at the top of the hill, there were dozens of surfers parked there. Someone said there's a competition. I watch through binoculars, though I can't really understand what's going on. I think I can see Joe, his red hair in a ponytail. The waves are huge. I take lots of photographs from the deck.

The new room is finished, and the new stairs. My room is the palest grey and white and I have a new chest of drawers and bookshelves. Rena Wooflie likes it and so do I. We're staying for the weekend. Mrs Thomas is feeding the cats.

A huge black cloud comes from the south and most of the surfers leave the water. There's a lightning flash over the sea and a roll of thunder.

'Better unplug everything,' says Alistair, and we go around unplugging the telly and phone connections. There's a sudden hailstorm and we stand at the sliding glass door to watch balls of ice bounce on the deck. The sky is very dark. Suddenly there's a blinding flash and a massive explosion. We are thrown off our feet. The fish-shaped plates that were on the plate shelf tumble and break on the table and floor. I find it hard to realise what's happening. I'm deaf and my eyes are momentarily blinded. My brain can't make sense of it all. Then I see that the huge tree about seven metres away has split down the middle and flaming splinters are flying into the garden and over the cliff into the sea. The tree has been struck by lightning. My ears are ringing. There are shouts from the beach – 'Help! Help!'

Alistair opens the glazed door and goes out onto the whitened deck and looks over the rail.

'Don't touch the metal.' Mum shrieks.

He says nothing, but runs down the deck steps, along the garden path, leaping over burning splinters of tree three metres long, towards the bottom gate onto the coast path. Mum is looking for her glasses, running around like a headless hen.

I step over broken china and glass, and go out onto the deck to see what's happening on the beach. Alistair has reached the rocks and is clambering over them. Two surfers lie face down in the water; others are pulling them out. I follow Alistair, running as fast as I can. I go around the still burning splinters, out the gate, which is hanging at a strange angle and run down the coast path. I scramble over the rocks down to the sea, wade through cold water and get to him as he is beginning to resuscitate someone.

'Let me through. I can do CPR,' I say. The small crowd of wet-suited boys moves aside and I see Alistair leaning over someone on the sand, feeling for a pulse.

'No pulse.'

Joe cries out, 'She's dead, she's dead!'

Alistair carries on compressing her chest.

'Come here,' he says. 'Take over from me.'

I go to his side and look down at the dead girl. It's Siobhan. He does the mouth to mouth, while I carry on with the chest compressions, five compressions to his one breath. I have to do it hard enough to compress the heart but not hard enough to fracture the ribs. Her ribs are very bendy – not like George.

'You're doing well, that's it, harder, a bit harder. Don't be frightened to press hard. One, two, three, four, five.'

There is another person unconscious further along the beach but someone is attending to him. We carry on for what seems like ages, but it's not working. She shows no signs of life.

A couple of boys are on their mobile phones. Two are holding their heads. One walks up and down in a daze. 'It feels like a bee sting,' he says. The tide is coming in fast and Alistair and another boy lift Siobhan's lifeless body and move her up the beach. Someone moves the unconscious boy too. We carry on with the resuscitation. I can't think of anything except the rhythm of my arms and hands as we try to save her life. My shoulders ache so much but I mustn't stop. Water laps at my feet. Heavy rain soaks me.

All I can think is – she can't die. She's only young, like me. She wants to live. She has a life to live. She mustn't die. Two boys and Alistair carry Siobhan and the unconscious boy away from the flooding tide again.

Suddenly, from across the rapidly narrowing beach a quad bike arrives and a man with a defibrillator rushes to us. I'm brushed aside as he gets to work. He cuts Siobhan's wetsuit down the front and puts the electrical contacts onto her flesh. I see her perfect small breasts, naked and beautiful.

And the dreadful thought comes into my head that my body will never be that beautiful, because of my scar. I am envious of this girl who could be dead. How awful of me! The pads are attached, one to her left breast and one to the side of it. He shocks her, but nothing happens. The machine shows no change to her stopped heart. He shocks her again and suddenly a heartbeat is visible on the monitor and Alistair calmly says there's a visible pulse in her neck. She's alive! There's a helicopter above us and it has difficulty landing on the narrowing space between the sea and the cliff. The noise is terrific and we have to cover our eyes because of the swirling sand. The other injured surfer is standing, with help from paramedics, though he looks very grey. I am suddenly aware of policemen, firemen and ambulance men on the beach. Siobhan is put on a stretcher and taken away with the grey-faced boy, who walks into the helicopter.

'Well done Gussie,' says Alistair, hugging me. We are surrounded by police, photographers, shivering surfers. I feel elated, adrenalin flooding my veins. I helped save someone's life. I can do it. You must feel like this all the time if you're a doctor or nurse, doing it every day.

The other surfers who were only slightly affected by the lightning have gone home. I asked one if he knew Phaedra and Troy and he said they had left the beach much earlier before the storm struck.

The foundations of the stone gatepost at the bottom of the garden have been exposed and the metal gate hinges have been blown out. There used to be a little wooden porthole there but it's been blown off and shattered.

Mum is making tea on the gas hob for the policemen – the electrics have blown and the telephone connections are blackened and blown out of the walls. A policeman says if anyone had been on the phone when the lightning struck they would have died. Mum's cleared up the broken china and glass and used Alistair's mobile phone to get a tree surgeon to come straight away. The tree is split from top to bottom down the middle and half of it hangs over the roof of the wooden cottage. We watch as the man climbs into the split bowl of the tree and begins sawing and attaching ropes to the branches. There's a strange smell in the air. The reporters and cameramen from TV have packed up and gone and the last policeman has finished his cup of tea and is leaving.

'Well, Doctor. That young woman was lucky you were here. She's be dead if it wasn't for you.'

'And Gussie,' Alistair says, holding me close. 'My assistant. Couldn't have done it without her.'

I feel ridiculously pleased.

'That lad though – he looked terrible – walking dead.'

Siobhan's parents have been informed.

The tree surgeon comes to the door with a dead pigeon. It looks asleep, its head drooping on its soft mauve breast.

'All right if I take it home?' He asks. 'I'll roast it with streaky bacon.'

The lightning-struck Monterey cypress has destroyed a large part of the garden, felling palms and banana plants, hydrangeas and bamboo. It looks so sad. There are huge splinters of wood everywhere. Rain falls. We go back to St Ives as there's no lighting or heating at the cottage. We find that the sound of the lightning striking the tree was heard in the town, and was thought to be a gas explosion. The town has power back now, though all the electricity was down for a while. Alistair stays the night.

Next day we are in all the papers, and on the radio and TV news. I am quite a celebrity.

'TEENAGE TRANSPLANT GIRL SAVES SCHOOL FRIEND'
'TRANSPLANT GIRL SAVES SURFER'
'LIGHTNING STRIKE – TWO IN INTENSIVE CARE'
'LIGHTNING HITS TWO SURFERS – A GP AND TEN-YEAR-OLD SCHOOLGIRL KEEP TEENAGER ALIVE FOR THIRTY MINUTES WAITING FOR A PARAMEDIC'

What headlines! But ten! Newspapers are always getting something wrong. Was it really only thirty minutes? It felt like hours.

I have written a poem about what happened:

The One Fatality

Afterwards, they found the one fatality –
A wood pigeon, which appeared
to be only sleeping, and which Nigel,
the tree-surgeon, roasted with streaky bacon,
parsnips, greens and a salsa of aubergine,
peppers and onion. Its meaty breast
had the subtle taste of saltpetre and brimstone.

Daddy phones and Mum proudly relates the rescue to him. At school, Bridget finds me and gives me a big hug.

'I thought I hated my sister, but when I heard what happened, I cried.'

'How is she?' I ask.

'She's in Intensive Care. Mum and my step-dad are with her.'

'Will she be okay, do they think?'

'Yeah, I think so. She's conscious, she can speak. They're doing lots of tests. I thought her insides would be fried. I was yellow with worry.'

'Yellow?'

'Yes, a bright yellow, like marigolds.'

'I think they're more orange than yellow.'

'Oh, well, orange then, I felt orange.'

'You are a strange child, Bridget,' I tell her and chase her round the playground and tickle her when I catch her.

People keep coming up to me and telling me how clever I am. Brett gives me a hug in front of several people. I can feel my cheeks burn.

'Goodonya Guss!'

High praise indeed!

Siobhan's mum comes to see my mum. They drink wine and cry a lot. I stay out of the way but can't escape a wine-flavoured kiss as she leaves.

My relations call – Fay sends a card with a painting of a magpie on, and says, 'Unbelievable, wonderful child. You have saved another's life. You will never be forgotten.'

If I have saved Siobhan's life (with the help of Alistair), am I responsible for the rest of her life? Or does she now have a responsibility to make something of her life? Whatever, we are somehow attached to each other, connected in some way. Like blood brothers – sisters.

Bubba and Rambo are next door with Mrs Thomas as usual. They've abandoned me. Mrs Thomas is looking more cheerful though, so they must be cheering her up. Perhaps I should formally give Bubba away to her? I'll ask Mum what she thinks.

Alistair is having a deck built on top of the tree-trunk – which is all that's left of the Monterey. It's shaped like a boat, with a prow over the cliff edge. The sun leaves the top deck about four thirty but stays on this deck for an hour later. Mum is happy to have more sunbathing time.

I keep thinking about Siobhan. I feel sort of responsible for her now I've helped to save her life. I want her to survive, with no damage to her brain or any other parts. I wonder if I could visit her in hospital. When she's out of Intensive Care. Mum says no. She'll only want to see her family.

At school I learn to play cricket. It's ace. I can hit the ball and catch it. I'm not afraid of it, even though it's hard. I tell our PE teacher that my grandma played in a men's team. She's impressed. I wear the England cap Alistair gave me and she doesn't mind.

I am more settled at school now. Everyone is friendlier and Siobhan returns and sits next to me in class. She has had her hair cut very short. I think it might have been shaved when she was in hospital. She looks frail. Not scary. She gives me a huge smile and a hug and says 'Thanks for saving my miserable life. I owe you.' Everyone claps and pats us on the back. It's embarrassing to get so much attention, but nice. She hauls me round with her at lunch-time, like I'm a reluctant dog on a string, and introduces me to all her friends.

'This is the girl who saved my life.' Siobhan remembers nothing about it apart from going into the water for the surf competition. Apparently most of the competitors had got out when they saw the storm coming. Siobhan and six other stragglers were just wading out of the sea when the lightning struck. It travelled down the tree, through the saturated cliff, into the water and up into the surfers. The others had been affected far less. One had cracked his head on his surf-board. Siobhan was very lucky that Alistair happened to be there that day. She has written him a card thanking him.

'I've been a bitch to you, Gussie, and I'm sorry,' she says.

Perhaps the electrical current that passed through her brain has made her a better person. Whatever, she is being perfectly nice to me, and to Bridget.

'We're going shopping in Penzance. Want to come?' she asks me. 'We' means Siobhan and her friend Leah.

'Shopping? Well, dunno, I'll have to ask Mum. How are you getting there?'

'Bus. It takes an age but it's fun. The driver's cool.'

Mum looks dubiously at me. 'You really want to go shopping?' She knows I hate shopping and have to be dragged to get clothes when I need anything new. She usually buys for me and if it doesn't fit, changes it. I'm not fussy about what I wear. Jeans, T-shirts, parkas, sneakers, camouflage jacket, cricket cap, DMs – I have all I need.

'Oh, come on Gussie. You don't have to buy anything, we just try things on for fun.'

'Why not? Okay. I'm in.'

Penzance is about an hour's bus ride through really pretty lanes full of cow parsley. We see brindled cattle and lots of pretty spotted horses, rabbits and several buzzards. I see a hare, tall-eared in the middle of a cropped field. Siobhan isn't interested in nature. She isn't sullen like I thought, though. She and Leah never stop talking – mostly about boys. She's 'in lust' with Joe, she says. I remember her small breasts and blush with embarrassment.

'Have you kissed him?'

'Snogged, you mean? Yeah, of course. He's ace at snogging.'

I'm out of my depth here.

'How about you and Brett?'

'Oh no. Nothing like that. We're just good friends.'

'I've seen the way you look at him,' says Leah, who is very mature looking, tall, with grey-green eyes, sooty lashes and dark curls.

'Yeah, well, he's going back to Australia soon, so...'

'Oh, shame. We'll have to find you another boyfriend,' says Shiv – she told me to call her that.

'No really. No thanks. I don't need one.' They laugh at me but I don't mind. It's not a sneering laugh, like it used to be, but more of a – 'oh, she's so young and innocent, isn't she sweet' sort of laugh. I don't get much chance to watch the world out the window as Shiv and Leah are talking to me all the time and mucking about. My chest hurts with laughing so much. In Penzance we go in all the clothes shops and try on all sorts of outrageous clothes and pretend to be older than we are. I buy some flat white canvas shoes with red polka dots. They look okay with jeans. Very okay. Siobhan buys a red cap with a large brim for herself and when I suggest that Bridget might like a blue one she actually buys that too.

'You're right. She'll look sweet in it.' I am astonished. I thought they didn't get on. Sibling relationships are very complicated and difficult for an only child to understand.

'Adorable,' I say, happily.

Leah and Shiv try on identical floral short skirts, very flirty and frilled. I think Leah looks better in it than Shiv, but Shiv insists she saw it first and wants it, so Leah can't have one too. Shiv says I'll look better in it than Leah, anyway, and suggests that I try it on. I do so, just for fun, and it doesn't look bad, I suppose, for a skirt. I don't buy it though. I don't want to have something that Shiv's got. She wouldn't like it. I buy a different skirt, with blue and white stripes. Mum will be amazed – her tomboy in a skirt! I wonder if Brett will like me in it? Leah buys a tight waistcoat and manages to look like she's eighteen.

Bridget is not happy that I am suddenly her sister's friend. I can almost see her turning viridian. Her eyes narrow like Charlie's when I'm petting Flo or Rambo or Bubba.

'Hi Bridget, is Shiv in?'

'She's out. Anyway, why do you like her now? You never used to.'

'She's changed. Haven't you noticed? She bought you that cap.'

'She's still Siobhan. I have to love her because she's my sister – half-sister actually – but I don't like her. She's always been horrible to me. She steals my things and hides them.'

'What things, when?'

'Well, she has anyway.'

'Has she lately?'

'No, I don't think so.'

'Well, then. You see – the lightning has changed her. The electrical charge to her brain made her a nicer person.'

'You don't *play* with me any more.'

'Come on, silly, let's play Barbies.'

She's mollified. What a pretty word – mollified.

Liam, who is Shiv's real brother, Bridget's half-brother, plays music loudly in his room and his stepfather yells at him to turn it down. Liam goes off in a strop, slamming the door. 'And don't slam the fucking door!' His stepfather shouts. He's built like a bull terrier and is almost as scary as one. Their mum is young and pretty, like Shiv. Bridget is mousy, like me, but her mum and Shiv have hair the colour of a blackbird's feathers, sleek and long and thick. Like I imagine Cinderella or the Sleeping Beauty to have.

'Is he your dad?' I ask Bridget.

'No, he's nobody's father. My dadda lives in Ireland, he has another family there. I'm going to run away and live with him when I've saved enough money.'

Poor little Bridget, I feel sad for her. I know what it's like to have no father. At least Alistair is nice and doesn't shout or swear at me.

CHAPTER TWENTY-ONE

ANOTHER LETTER FROM Natalie's mother:

Dear Gussie,

You asked me how my daughter died. Natalie always rode her bicycle to work. She was a very health-conscious girl. That morning it was raining and the road was slippery, I believe. A car hit her at a junction. She died of her multiple injuries. She had always carried a donor card and as well, had told me and her father that she was registered as a donor. When she was on life-support her wish was in our minds and we had no hesitation in supporting her desire. It was what she would have wanted. It is astonishing that her heart and lungs are giving you a new life. Bless you, dear, and all the best for the rest of your life. I forgot to say that Natalie was engaged to be married. Her fiancé is white, Scottish. We are from Jamaica. He – James – often comes to visit. Yes – we have lost a daughter but gained a son. And maybe, with you a new half-daughter?

Natalie's spirit is still here with me. She loved her life and I hope you love yours.

Best wishes and blessings, Abigail Bridges

Mum and I seem to be crying again. But I'm glad I know who my donor was and I hope that they will have some gladness that her organs are still working inside someone who appreciates them and their loss.

I wonder why Mrs Bridges didn't send me an email, it's so much easier than writing a letter, finding an envelope and stamp and posting it. Mum said it's probably because it's such an important subject and she wanted me to be able to keep it. I suppose email is more for small messages that can be deleted, chucked, not treasured. Electronic postcards.

At the car-boot sale I find several postcards with interesting messages:

Herne Bay, 1909:
Will you kindly send me my galoshes,
I think I left them on the piano –
Much love from Auntie Emma

Truro, 1913:
Quite forgot to say this morning about
Mirtle, rub a little butter on her nose.
Mother says there is nothing better.
Hope this finds you all well –
With love, Carrie

Kent, 1914:
Will you kindly have washer put in
lavatory overflow pipe as soon as
possible as the garden is always
wet, and it is most inconvenient.

Newquay, 1965:
Dear Mum, we arrived safe after slow journey down.

*I thought perhaps an angel on the bedspread
might look nice.
Got your letter, see you next week.
Love, Chris*

I feel as if I am looking into history through the odd things people wrote. One thing I have noticed is that the writers often refer to seeing the person they are writing to later that day, so the postal service must have been brilliant. We have one delivery a day and that doesn't arrive until lunchtime.

Note: A basking shark off Peregrine Point, about four metres long, moving in circles. The sea is calm and we see it very clearly. I take pictures. But we don't actually see the gaping mouth, so can't be sure it is definitely a basking shark. It's long and slender, and it has a dorsal fin about halfway along its back.

From my bedroom window I hear a small boy sneeze in the back lane and say to his daddy, 'My head exploded.'

I wish I could still see life as a small child sees it. Everything new every second. Life does amaze – clouds, the sea, always new, always exciting.

Mum is less stressed these days – doesn't watch me every second, waiting for me to die. I still live for the day though, make the most of each experience.

Will my breasts ever grow? I'm as flat as a cowpat. I wear my new skirt with black tights – Mum raises her eyebrows but Alistair says I look very pretty. Brett's coming over. I put on Mum's concealer over my blotchy complexion, and find a plain black T-shirt to go with the skirt. Brett doesn't notice the skirt.

Well, he does.

He casts a disapproving eye over my clothes.

'You aren't birding in that, are you?' he says.

'Of course not, I was just about to change,' I lie. 'Anyway, don't you like it?'

'I prefer your usual clothes.'

He means my combat gear. I think I look like an army cadet. But it's more comfortable than a skirt, and I can climb and run without showing my knickers. It's hard work behaving like a lady.

We walk along the coast path and find a lizard sunbathing on the dry-stone wall. It scuttled away like a ghost, one moment there, the next gone.

'You aren't really friends with Siobhan are you?'

'She's fun,' I say defensively.

'She's not to be trusted.'

He would say that, as she wasn't faithful to him.

We go to Man's Head and then on to the Clodgy, and hunker down with a rock to lean against. There are all sorts of gold and green lichens and tiny flowering succulents growing over it, like the most beautiful miniature rock garden. We don't say much to each other, though I am aware of time hurrying by and he'll be gone soon, by the end of the summer term. It's a sad happiness I feel, being with him now. Bittersweet. I don't want to feel too close to him, because I know I'll feel bereft when he leaves. Like when Precious died.

Note: I'm getting better at recognising bird song and habits – the sad piping of the oystercatcher, the flash of red, black and white as they take off together; the harsh low notes of the black-backs; the squeaking high notes of the black-headed gulls and terns. It's familiarity that does it – I learn by seeing and hearing several times. Books are good for identifying birds I haven't seen before, but nothing beats actually being out there with them, noticing the way they fly and interact. For example, the way that goldfinches flutter and skip around in the sky, dancing on air, singing all the time, chattering prettily. And the way that blackbirds hop and skip along the earth, and chase off smaller ground-feeders, birds like robin and dunnock.

Bridget feels abandoned, though I am not abandoning her. And Mum finds Shiv untrustworthy.

'Why do you think that?'

'Just a gut feeling. She doesn't look me in the eye.'

'But I like being her friend. I'm meeting loads more people now.'

'We'll see,' she says enigmatically.

Siobhan is the prettiest girl in the class, that's for sure. All the boys fancy her. To be seen with her is an accolade, like being seen with a movie star.

Phaedra, who I hardly ever see, warns me to stay away from Siobhan.

'Why?'

'She's a tramp.'

'How is she?'

'She flirts with anything – she'd flirt with an orang-utan. She's just not cool.'

I heard from Bridget, that her sister (half-sister) had been out with a boy in Phaedra's band, who is seventeen. She stole him from another girl. I don't care. I'm having fun being Shiv's friend. Everyone says hello to me in the school corridor and in the playground. When Brett goes, I'll need friends.

Bridget says – 'Just because you saved her life doesn't mean you are part of her life.' Poor little Bridget. She's too young to understand.

Summer term is being good to me. Mum and Alistair come

to see me play cricket. My running isn't brilliant yet. I get to bowl – Alistair has shown me how to bowl a Chinaman – a left hand off break, which means turning from the off to the leg. It's a wrist spinner as opposed to a finger spinner. I get three wickets. I'm the girl of the match. Or would be if we had such a thing.

On Saturday I am just about to go out with Siobhan around town when Brett phones to see if I'll go birding.

'Sorry, Brett. I've promised to do something else.'

'No worries.'

We walk around the harbour, Shiv, Leah and me, window-shopping at all the clothes shops and ogling the boys on their skateboards.

'Come on, let's play the machines,' says Leah, pulling on my arm. I'm between her and Shiv and they are heading for the amusement arcade.

'I'm not allowed.'

'Why?' says Shiv. 'Don't be such a baby. It can't hurt to look.'

Several boys home in on us – or rather, Shiv – like bees to honey. Leah is quite tall and strong with blonde wispy hair in a ponytail. She's thirteen and looks much older. Shiv wears low-cut jeans and a cropped white top, showing off her belly button stud.

'Who's the geek kid?' says a boy with blond highlights and a skateboard under one arm. He's smoking a roll-up.

'She saved my life. Be sweet,' says Shiv, and I glow with pride. He blows smoke into her face and she kisses him. I'm embarrassed and look away. I thought she was going out with Joe? Shiv and Leah light up cigarettes and Shiv offers hers to me.

'You've got to be joking! I'm not messing up my new lungs!'

'Okay, baby Guss. I forgot.'

A few of the skateboarders join us. I recognise one or two from school. We fool around for a while, playing the machines in the middle of the noise, the music, the crowds. It's so exciting. But it all goes wrong. Someone smashes a Coke bottle into a machine and glass shatters. A man shouts at us and we take off, broken glass crackling under our shoes.

'I know you! You're banned!' He shouts after us and we run giggling along the harbour, dashing between ambling holidaymakers with north country accents. It starts to rain hard and I lose the others. It doesn't matter. I lean over the harbour rail, watching ghosts shiver under the water. I go home, wet through but elated by… belonging to Shiv's crowd, being popular, being part of *life*! How about that? Banned after my first time in the arcade! I've gone from a nonentity to being notorious. I hope Mum doesn't find out.

CHAPTER TWENTY-TWO

'That's quite a dress you almost have on.' Gene Kelly,
An American in Paris, 1951

SHIT! I THINK I'm getting a cold. Mum keeps me away from school, wraps me in cottonwool practically!

'What were you doing staying out in the rain without a coat?' She's cross.

'You don't get colds by being wet. I didn't get ill when I was helping resuscitate Siobhan, did I?'

'Shut up, you'll swallow the thermometer.'

I stay in bed and the cats join me, delighted for the excuse to lie around all day on blankets. And would you believe it? The sun has come out and it's very summery, and I can't enjoy it. Our roof gulls are settling down to a carefree middle age now they are chickless, and we only see them for a short while each day. They land and shuffle, their wings closed across their backs. I still hear the occasional juvenile flying over, its shrill trembling call like a squeaky gate.

Mum was going out with Alistair to get some curtain material for the cliff cottage, but she's put it off. She's keeping an eye on me.

Being in bed is a wonderful excuse to read, even though my nose is running and I have to keep blowing it.

I have read all of Scott Fitzgerald and don't know what

to try next. Usually when I'm not well I fall back on old favourites like the Swallows and Amazons books, or Jack London, but now I want more of a challenge. Perhaps I'll stick to poetry. Alistair brought over a few of his collection. He likes Billy Collins best. He's American, still alive and very witty as well as profound. I love his one about a wet dog never being welcome, and he guesses even in a thousand years, maybe on another planet, to alien creatures, a wet dog still won't be welcome. I'm writing a poem about my white cockerel. He was my first pet and lived with Grandma and Grandpop. They kept chickens. I'm afraid they killed him and roasted him and I ate a wing before I realised which chicken it was.

White Cockerel

I called him King.
He was a gentle despot

caressing his fowls
with angel wings.

The feathered sheikh
clucked in my arms

as we toured his realm
and chose fattest goose-

berries, sweetest rasp-
berries, found the tiny

pullet's eggs. He loved
me with his yellow eyes,

stroked me with the frilly
nippleflesh of his red comb.

It wasn't until I had eaten
a crispy wing and the tenderest
slice of breast, that I asked,
'Which is it?'

Then I screamed.

I've found another that I started ages ago, and I think I've
finished it now:

Raining Cats and Dogs

It rains for days until drains
are blocked with Birman and Poodles
and we paddle in Pekinese pups.

Gutters overflow with Goldendoodles;
roofs sag under the weight of wet Water Spaniels
sodden Shih Tzu and sopping Schnauzer.

At every window the pitter-patter
of Whippets and Pomeranians,
a spatter of Singapura and Sphinx.

Trees tumble under a torrent of tabbies,
Siamese and Terriers, Chow Chow,
Chihuahuas, miserable Manx.

We drown in daily downpours of ginger toms,
Dalmations and Doberman

Dachshunds and dank Great Danes.
Umbrellas are bowed and broken
by Borzoi and Beagle, the steady precipitation
of Persians who frown even more bad-
temperedly than usual,
the splash, drip, drizzle of Lhaso Apso.

I found all those dog names in a book. Lhaso Apso! Isn't that gorgeous?

I'm going to show it to Alistair. He wants a dog, but Mum is horrified at the idea. She thinks he'll bring it here and frighten the cats and poo in the garden – the dog, not Alistair.

I am going to write some more poems based on silly sayings like Raining Cats and Dogs.

I'm not out of the high-risk time for acute rejection so I'm still on heavy dose immunosuppressants. Mum's monitoring my temperature and lung function every day. So far my temperature's been stable. If it goes up I'll have to go back into hospital and go on big doses of steroids and antibiotics and physio again. I really don't want to go on steroids again, they make my face moon-shaped. Oh shit! Wish I hadn't got so drenched and chilled. Wish I hadn't gone with Siobhan and Leah to the arcade. At least Mum doesn't know what I was doing that day.

CHAPTER TWENTY-THREE

IT'S OFFICIAL – I have a respiratory infection. I had to go for an urgent outpatient appointment for assessment and sit miles away from the other patients – because of the risk of infection to me, not them. Temperature is up, lung function down. Mum is advised to get me back to the transplant unit ASAP.

In hospital again. A single room.

Have had another assessment to make sure I'm not rejecting again. But they aren't sure, so they're treating me for suspected rejection and chest infection. I'm on intravenous antibiotics.

Don't feel too good. Nightmares. Chills.

Pull down my pyjama sleeves over my wrists, my pyjama trouser legs over my ankles, in a feeble attempt to warm up. Would love a hot water bottle but am not allowed one – Health and Safety? What crap! Have to have three days of intravenous methylprednisolone for the acute rejection and then wait for test results to improve. The physio, Dolores, remembers me.

'It's Gorgeous Gussie!'

She gets me to cough properly to shift sputum.

Mum stays in a hospital flat, but Alistair has gone back to Cornwall. Mum has these worry lines between her eyes. It's always an anxious time when things start going wrong. I feel rather weak and wobbly just now. Forgot to bring Rena Wooflie. She'll be cross. She always comes to hospital with me. I miss having her to cuddle.

I feel awful – no energy even to read a book, so Mum reads to me from a Rumer Godden, *Kingfishers Catch Fire*. I'm sure it's good but I keep dropping off. Where does that saying come from – dropping off what? The edge of consciousness, perhaps? She has to whisper the words because sounds hurt my head.

There wasn't time before we left to phone to let Shiv know what's happened, or Brett, only the Darlings and Marigold, but Mum has since phoned Claire and asked her to let the school know what's happened.

I have a different room this time – no friendly spider on the ceiling. No scary crow outside. There's an empty bird-feeder stuck to the outside of the window and Mum gets some birdseed for it. It'll take a few days before any birds discover the new food source.

It's been four days and no birds yet. I haven't met any of the other in-patients. I have to remain in this room and not have any contact with anyone except Mum and the staff, who all wear masks. I feel like I'm a leper, but it's for my own protection. I know that. Still, it's a drag. There's a telly but it makes my headache worse. There's a willow outside the window and I like the whooshing sound that the narrow leaves make. My sense of smell has gone, and my appetite. I get a shock when I see my face in the mirror – as I suspected, I've got a moon-face. I have to keep reminding myself that

I am lucky to be alive at all, and not to worry too much about these minor setbacks. I just wish Mum wouldn't look so worried. It makes me worried too.

'I can't help it, darling,' she says. 'It should get easier, but it doesn't. I feel so helpless. I could stand it if it was me who was ill, but not you.' We hold each other, our wet cheeks rubbing together. 'I thought it would be better after the transplant, but it isn't. Sorry, darling.'

I get a card from Brett. Hayley has had to go back to Australia suddenly because Brett's grandmother has had a stroke. I hope *he* doesn't leave England before I get a chance to see him again.

No card from Shiv, but a postcard from Bridget sending me love and prayers. She's discovered religion and she's praying for everyone, including her sister, who, she says, is a lost cause and she's sure she'll go to Hell. Apparently she's reverted to being horrible, hiding her stuff and stealing her pocket money (if Bridget can be believed).

Claire has written to Mum and sends love from them all.

Mrs Thomas is happy to feed the cats. If I have to stay longer than a week or so, they'll go to the Darlings as before, except for Bubba and Rambo, who Marigold is eager to keep with her. It's not fair – my cats are deserting me. Rats leaving a sinking ship. That's how I feel. I'm a sinking ship, creaking beams, filling with water, about to capsize or flounder, or whatever ships do – sink. That's how I feel. Sinking. New antibiotics start to work... hurray!

A letter from Gabriel with a leaflet describing his latest love – carnivorous plants:

PITCHER PLANTS. These are the most simple trap. They

produce a jug-like formation hanging from the end of a leaf (nepenthes). Other varieties produce a long tube-like formation which grows from the base of the plant (sarracenias).

Both varieties have lids to stop them filling up with rainwater. A sweet smell comes from around the rim of the pitcher and the underside of the lid to attract insects. When the insect lands on the rim it finds that it is quite slippery and the insect usually falls into the pitcher and drowns, the dead insect is then digested by the enzymes that the plant produces.

VENUS FLYTRAP. People still do not fully understand how a flytrap closes. It does not have a nervous system or muscles or tendons. Scientists think that it moves from some type of fluid pressure activated by an electrical impulse that runs through each lobe. The flytrap only digests the soft inner parts of the fly. It leaves the outer part which blows away when the trap opens again.

Note: Flytrap facts: If the flytrap detects an insect it shuts in less than a second. It takes from 5 to 12 days for the Venus flytrap to digest a fly. It digests its prey with very much the same digestive juices as we do. It also has antiseptic juices to stop the fly from rotting. Some mature Venus flytraps can eat small frogs!

CHAPTER TWENTY-FOUR

Note: Feral London pigeons aren't as pretty as our Cornish pigeons (quite a few are disabled by a missing foot) but they still remind me of Grandma – a similar waddle, head bobbing forward. They all look like elderly ladies, slightly grumpy, as if they are worrying about what to cook for supper. There's one in the willow who looks like she's carrying lots of heavy shopping, waiting for a late bus in the rain and wishing she had brought an umbrella. (How do so many of them lose a foot? They surely can't all have caught their feet in traps?) It would be so cool to be able to speak in Birdspeak.

'Excuse me asking, Mr Pigeon, but how did you lose your foot?'

'Well, it was like this, young woman. It was the Great Pigeon War. I was in the Battle of Trafalgar Square, when all the pigeons were banned. A few of us fought back. We'd been feeding there for hundreds of years. It was our territory. My great-great-great-great-great-great... whatever, my ancestors had been shitting on Nelson since he was placed on his column. The tourists took photos of us and fed us bread. We didn't really like their white sliced loaves – no sustenance in them, you know, but there you are, we obliged them. We were part of the English Tourist Industry. Unpaid volunteers. And they turned on us. Sent the old enemy in – the dreaded falcons. I lost twenty-four cousins to them.

Starvation was their next weapon. Stopped feeding us.
How cruel is that?

'SCRABBLE?'
'Penny a point.'
'Wretched child, you're winning all your inheritance.'
'Might as well have it now,' I say.

I go from euphoria to deepest despair. I have been told many times to expect these emotional highs and lows when I'm on high doses of steroids – deliriously happy when the doses first kick in and then emotional as they drop – but it feels so real at the time. Every time I see the physios I think of Precious, and I get a hurting lump in my throat.

I've just remembered something he told me about the song of the mourning dove. It sings – Poor me, poor me, poor me. My mother is dead, my father is dead, my brothers and sisters are dead, poor me. And I wonder about his father – is he in prison, is he alive? Where are his mother and sisters? Are they alive?

Katy comes to see me. She was one of my specialist post-transplant nurses when I was recovering from the operation. She thinks I have grown upwards as well as outwards. Soo Yung, a pretty specialist nurse, who was here before, has moved to another hospital. It's like a small town, the hospital, where most of the staff know each other, and absences, illnesses and death are noticed and felt by the community. There's even a chapel, and a shop and Post Office. We patients are only visitors, temporary inhabitants. Like holidaymakers in St Ives. Here for a short time, trying to fit in with the life of the town.

I know none of the town's new visitors, only the long-term inhabitants – the staff.

Mum goes out for the afternoon and evening with her friend Mimi. She Deserves Time Off. She Hasn't had her Hair Done and she Needs a Good Curry. Daddy comes to see me. He smells nice – sort of decadent/glamorous, like chocolate and champagne, and he wears a beautiful dark grey shirt. He brings chocolates, for the nurses and me, and says that the exhibition is definitely happening in the winter sometime.

Three of my photographs will be shown, and a few of his, but mostly it'll be a showcase for Amos Hartley Stevens, my great-grandfather. Three generations of photographers in one family.

He says he has completely restyled his apartment and wants us to come for supper to see it before we go back to Cornwall. I wonder if he discovered the tear in his black mosquito net, but don't ask in case I have to explain. He still isn't aware that I had Beelzebub living there for several weeks and that it was she who was responsible for the damage to his cream suede sofa-bed and his rug. What the head doesn't know the heart doesn't grieve over – or something like that. One of Grandma's favourite expressions. She said that when she dropped the roast beef on the kitchen floor, and picked it up and served it.

I've now missed two and a half weeks of school. But I am improving. I'm recovered from the chest infection. That's what it was, not acute rejection. I wish I had brought Rena Wooflie. Alistair hasn't been able to get away or I could have asked him to bring her. I know she's not alive, like a cat, but she has been a constant companion since I was small, and I can almost believe she has a personality. I feel like she's much older than me. She looks wise and calm, like my grandma. Stern sometimes, but she's always right. She keeps me on the straight and narrow. Another of Grandma's expressions. It means I must behave properly, not be rude, always be polite and kind to others. She's a bit like Flo. Keeps me on my toes (another foot metaphor for my collection). Thought of another too – my heart is in my boots! A heart and foot metaphor.

The schoolroom has been out of bounds until today. I used the computer for a while. There are two other people in there but I don't really want to get to know them, in case... anyway, I'm leaving hospital tomorrow.

Daddy's for supper – Mimi and Willy from upstairs are there. Three bottles of champagne! Steak and salad, strawberries and ice-cream.

His flat – he calls it an apartment these days – is painted Pigeon Grey and Antique White with lots of stainless steel and squashy sofas in black or cream leather. No mosquito net. A new bed with surround sound, and lots of cowskin rugs. I keep thinking I can smell cowpats, but I say nothing.

The big news is that Willy and Mimi are getting married later this year and we are invited. Mum is pleased to have an excuse to buy new clothes. I'll have to have Something Decent too. Not a dress, I hope.

Daddy hasn't got a girlfriend at the moment, he says, and anyway I'm the love of his life.

Home again! Cats all over me – except for Bubba, who has definitely deserted me for Marigold Thomas. She is apologetic – Mrs Thomas, not Beelzebub. But I am making it formal. I have given the kitten up for adoption. Rambo lives in both houses, not quite realising that Bubba is now Bubba Thomas and not Bubba Stevens. Actually, she is now Barbara, not Bubba – Mrs Thomas couldn't cope with the Beelzebub idea and has always thought of her as Barbara.

Perhaps the kitten will grow into her name, not be a little devil, but be sorry like the girl in the song 'Barbara Allen'. The original Barbara Allen was a flirt and horrid to William, the boy who loved her, but regretted it when he died and she then stopped being cold-hearted.

I spend the rest of the day humming the tune and singing the only words I know of it:

> In Scarlet town where I was born
> There was a fair maid dwellin',
> Made every youth cry 'Well-a-day'
> Her name was Barbara Allen.

And there's a bit where he's ill and she's called to see him and she says, 'Young man I think you're dyin'.' How cold-hearted was that! I think I might end up calling the kitten Barbie. She is a bit of a Barbie – pretty and not very bright.

I am having a day off school to recover from the journey – five hours on the train. First Class again – as Mum said, 'I could get used to this.'

Shiv? She hasn't been in touch. Why?

Brett comes to see me. Hayley is still with her mother in Australia. He has brought me an interesting book for my collection, *Seashore and Weather Lore* by Mildred Swannell. We read bits of it out to each other:

The Cormorant's Dirty Nests

Of all the breeding places of sea birds, this of the cormorant is surely the foulest and most evil-smelling. Odds and ends of fish lie about, the nests are wet and dirty, and amid this noisomeness the naked, blue-black babies clamour for food. They are fed in the strangest way; their parents stand before them while the youngsters thrust their long necks far down the capacious gullets and help themselves to the partly digested contents.

I love the old-fashioned language and interesting words: noisomeness! It doesn't mean full of noise, which is what I thought it meant. It means smelly. Well, noisome means smelly, so I suppose noisomeness is the state of being smelly. Like happiness is the state of being happy and joyfulness is the state of being joyful. Or is it simply joy?

The cormorant is a quaintly shaped, clumsy-looking bird, about a yard in length, and, for most of the year, clothed in sombre black, except for the white throat. But early in spring, just before courting time, the male puts on wedding garments, which consist of the addition of a crest of black and white hair-like feathers and a white patch on his thighs; the only coloured spots are the emerald green eyes, which can be seen when the observer is close at hand.

And here's something about a bird I've never seen:

The Storm Petrel

Even inland children have heard of 'Mother Carey's Chickens'. though few have seen them, and many living by the sea are not familiar with the little birds, simply because they do not know for what to look. Mother Carey's Chickens is the name given by sailors to a small bird about the size of a sparrow, clothed all in black, except for a conspicuous white patch on the rump and upper tail coverts. Another name for it is the Stormy Peter, and both names tell something of its habits. Mother Carey is supposed to be a storm witch, who, when she rides about, is accompanied by numbers of the little black birds – hence called her chickens. The word 'petrel' means Little Peter, in reference to St Peter's attempt to walk on the waves. The stormy petrel does have the appearance of walking on the sea, for, as it flies very low it lets its webbed feet paddle in the water; also it is more in evidence in stormy weather. As it is not easy to see objects near the water, even a little way out from the shore, this may be one of the reasons why its name has caught the imagination, while the bird itself is less familiar.

The book is No. VI of Pitman's Nature Series for Juniors.

The storm petrel nests in old rabbit holes in sand dunes and rock crevices and feed their young on oily, fatty foods.

As darkness deepens, faint sounds can be heard from the burrows – the little ones calling for food, and home fly the parents with crops full of oil, which is poured into the young ones' beaks through tubes opening at the nostrils and which may be seen as small protuberances on the upper mandibles.

'Have you ever seen a storm petrel?'

'Don't reckon so. We have lots of pelicans back home. They're huge birds, comic – you'd like 'em, I reckon.'

He's talking about Australia as 'Home', I notice.

'Perhaps we can go to the Island next time there's bad weather and watch for petrels?' he says. I nearly say that he'll be back Home by the time the autumn storms come, but I say nothing. I want to pretend that this summer will never end and Brett will never leave. I ought to be making the most of my time with him, but I'm not relaxed with him any more, I suppose I'm preparing myself for when he's gone. It's like grieving before someone's dead.

Mum and I spend time in the garden; she does a bit of weeding, and I groom the cats. Bubba comes into our garden and I groom her too. She has lots of fleas. I don't think Mrs Thomas can have been combing her. She (Bubba, not Mrs Thomas), and all the cats lounge around in the sun. They missed me, I think. They have followed me everywhere since I've been home.

It's quiet up here at the top of the hill, though I can hear a boatman calling out on his megaphone – 'Seal Island, anyone for Seal Island?' I think if I ever have to leave here for good, that's the human sound I'll remember most fondly. The other sounds are the sea and the wind. Never the same, but always there in the background – and sometimes in the foreground, overwhelming every other sensation. Scary to be almost surrounded by sea. I have a healthy respect for it. I have no desire to surf, like Phaedra and Troy or Siobhan and Joe. I'm too scared of its power. So many people are drowned in Cornwall, swept away by rogue waves.

In our garden the pond is bordered by shells and pebbles, the apple tree is crowded with tiny fruit and there are lots of young salad leaves and herbs growing in a wooden trough.

Mrs Thomas comes out, hangs out her washing, props the line with a long wooden pole and sits on the step. Mum has offered to do her garden, as she is too old to cope with the digging and weeding. Mum doesn't say that of course. Mrs Thomas has accepted the offer. Mum loves gardening and has been itching to get at the neglected patch since we moved here. In no time she has cut the grass, demolished the broken bench and tidied up a bit. She's never happier than when she has a pair of secateurs in her hand. (Unless it's a glass of whisky.)

Alistair has bought us a bee box, a tit nesting box and a bat box. He's nailed the bat box up high under the eaves of the roof, the tit box lower down but near the ivy that grows up the front wall, because they like cover, and the bee box sits facing south in among the flowers. I would like a robin nesting box, but they like to nest low down, and he says they would be vulnerable to cat attack anywhere in our garden.

The nesting boxes might be occupied next spring. He says he's ordered lots of them for his cliff house. He's also very generously supplied us with large bags of birdseed and sunflower seeds for the feeders. Sparrows chatter in the bushes and starlings whistle and click on the telegraph wire outside my window. The roof gulls are on holiday.

Claire and Gabriel came yesterday evening and stayed for fish and chips. St Ives has much nicer fish and chips than London. That's because the fish comes from the same postcode as the fish and chip shop. Gabriel said he had copied the information about his carnivorous plants from the Internet. Claire says it's brilliant for research, though you can't always believe everything that's on it. Gabriel loves me and wants to marry me. He gave me a ring he'd made of copper wire.

'Gabriel, I'm happy you love me. And I love you.'

He smiles broadly.

'But we can't marry, because we're related. It's not allowed. Or anyway, it's not wise, because our genes are too similar. Know what I mean?'

He looks sad and I hug him.

'I'll always love you, Gabe. Just can't marry you, you know?'

'Can I have your pickled onion?' he asks.

'May I, and please,' I say and give it to him.

After school I phone Shiv's house but her mum's boyfriend answers and says she isn't there. No one's there but him. He sounds drunk and bad-tempered. At five o'clock in the afternoon!

Back to school. I still look like a hamster. When I complained about my appearance to Mum she said that Grandma used to say to her, 'Who's going to look at you?' Mum's not that insensitive. She says she loves me no matter what I look like. When I look dismayed she hugs me and laughs.

'Gussie, you're the most beautiful girl in the world,' she lies and we both laugh.

Shiv's not at school. Haven't seen Bridget either. I wonder where they've gone? Leah doesn't know and says she doesn't care.

I am totally left behind in every lesson. I've lost too much study time. I hate school! I thought it was going to be so much fun and it really isn't. No one has time to explain anything to me. Maths is a nightmare. It might as well be in Martian, and I can't cope. I get tearful in class but try to hide it. At least we have cricket in the afternoon. I score a couple of runs and get cheers from my team for my efforts. It feels great when they do that. I wish my grandma could see me following in her footsteps. Perhaps I'll be a professional cricketer. I could get to be as good as Brian Lara, and be made a knight – or dame, probably. Dame Augusta Stevens. Sounds good. I wouldn't need Maths.

No one seems to know what's happened with Shiv

and Bridget. Liam's missing too. I'll ask Brett if he knows anything.

He doesn't. Says he hasn't heard a thing. The mystery deepens. Has the layabout piss-head boyfriend murdered them all? Buried them under the concrete yard? Should someone tell the police? Or are they off on holiday or visiting a sick gran? What's happened to Spike? I know the poor suffering fish are still there, but maybe they belong to the boyfriend. Should I phone the RSPCA about them? They are probably all dead by now. Oh dear, poor fish. I should have said something before. Like in those predictable action movies – the fish bite the dust, kick the bucket, fall off the perch, whatever. Get their aquarium shot to pieces and end up drowning in oxygen on the floor usually.

CHAPTER TWENTY-FIVE

'Run! Forrest, run!' Robin Wright, *Forrest Gump*, 1994

GIRLS' CRICKET SQUAD:
Josephine da Silva (Captain)
Lisa Innes (Vice-Captain)
Gaynor Sutherland
Chloe Jenkyns
Sahara Symons
Taylor Thomas
Caitlin Sidebottom
Kelly Craze
Opal Shah
Halle Turner
Georgia Cousins
RESERVES:
Nancy Humphries
Gussie Stevens – me!
Emma Eddy

JO DA SILVA is brilliant. She's going to play for Cornwall one day – so says our sports teacher, Miss Payntor – (we call her Pain). Jo's seventeen and will leave soon for sixth form college, but it's a huge honour to be in her squad. She chose me out of several girls who were up for the place. I'm the youngest and smallest, not the fastest or best, but I can hit the ball and catch it. Lots of girls are afraid of it because it's hard, but if you hold your hands in the right position and gather it into your body it doesn't hurt. I like fielding. It's such a joy to run and throw myself around. It feels good to get bruised and scraped. I appreciate my body and what it is capable of now. My operation scars are not important. In fact, they are like the bruises and scabs I get from playing – badges of honour.

I'm playing tennis too. Not so good with backhands – I have to use both hands – but I enjoy it. And I love rounders.

So, I'm hopeless academically, but quite good at sports. How ironic is that? No one is impressed by the books I've read. Our English teacher hadn't heard of Mary Webb or Rumer Godden or Paul Gallico. I'm shocked. But when I tell Mum she says they are probably too busy reading more modern books and I mustn't become an intellectual snob.

There's nets after school, in the same field where we watched Alistair play cricket last summer. A far view over the bay – Hayle and Gwithian and Godrevy Lighthouse.

Note: Swallows swoop low, almost scraping a groove in the grass with their scimitar wings. Crows complain in the black trees. Three brown horses doze in the lower field, necks arched like swans, muzzles to the earth. On the wind I smell the sea and grass. A high buzzard mews.

I walk back down town with Nancy and Emma. We're all excited about tomorrow's match against Truro Girls. It's an away match, and we'll travel by bus. No idea if I'll get chosen, but I'm in with a chance. Emma is a better bowler than me and Nancy is a solid fielder. My batting might get me in. We're all in with a chance.

They have no idea what's happened to Shiv. There's a rumour that their mother left home with another man and the children were taken into care, but I can't believe that. Another rumour is that she left her boyfriend because he was hitting her and took the children with her.

I've packed my cricket gear and my England cap for luck. I'm so excited!

Rambo doesn't appear for tea. I assume he's at Mrs Thomas's house with Bubba, so I don't worry. But she hasn't seen him. We call to him along the back lane and the front path, and on the hill, but there's no sign. Now I'm worried. He always turns up for food and never strays far from home – he's a gentle, unadventurous, home-loving cat. A neutered tom, he's not a brave adventurer, or a fighter.

He does come home later that night. The telly's off and I hear a low, mewing cry and open the door for him. I hold him while Mum cleans him up. He has a bloody face. Half his tongue is hanging off and he's lost most of his teeth. One ear is bloody, badly torn. Both front paws are badly hurt. He kneels on his elbows – the forepaws are paralysed. He can't eat or drink.

In the morning I phone Miss Payntor and say I can't make the match as I have to take my cat to the vet. She sounds cross. I am not reliable, she says. This is my chance to play for the school. I shouldn't let a pet come before the honour of the school.

'I'm sorry,' I say.

'I'll take him on my own, Gussie, you must go to the match.' Mum tries to persuade me.

'No, he needs me there too,' I say.

The emergency vet shakes his head. He says Rambo's severed tongue will eventually fall off, so he probably won't be able to wash himself again and he's doubtful whether Rambo will regain the use of his forepaws. He asks if we want him to put Rambo out of his misery.

'Are there internal injuries?' asks Mum.

'No, I think he must have been hit by a vehicle, but only his front quarters seem to be affected.'

Mum is as tearful as me. She looks at me and I shake my head firmly.

He injects Rambo with antibiotics and we take him home. I feed him watery milk with an eye dropper. He gulps thirstily, dribbling down his front. He'll survive, I know he will. His round limpid eyes gaze at me, dark and deep. Charlie and Flo sniff at him and back away. They can smell The Dreaded Vet: antiseptic, clean, medical. That smell means pain and fear. I know how they feel.

CHAPTER TWENTY-SIX

I CLEAN THE poor cat using a bit of old white muslin curtain, wetting it, squeezing it out and dabbing at his face. He purrs. But I do know that purring in sick cats can mean that they are anxious, not happy. I stroke him and talk to him, tell him I love him and he'll feel better soon. Mum gives him the antibiotics. I'm no good at holding his mouth open. His poor damaged mouth, bloody still. Only two teeth left. He sucks at the eyedropper. Some goodness goes down. Most drips down his front. I clean up the stickiness. I do the usual grooming too, combing his tabby fur. No fleas. That's one good thing. His front paws are lifeless, the nerves damaged, but he attempts to walk. It's painful to watch. His 'elbows' are raw. It's amazing that he managed to get home in that state. Where could it have happened? Hardly any cars go down the back lane. Did he go down the hill?

Bubba comes in the cat flap and stops when she sees Rambo. Her fur stiffens, her back arches. She hisses. She gradually gets closer to him and sniffs suspiciously. She licks his lowered head. She's mothering him. He's purring, they're both purring. She licks him thoroughly, probably disgusted at his poor state of hygiene, or perhaps she understands that he can't clean himself, and automatically does it for him – a maternal instinct. Whatever, it's great that he has found a little nurse. She's his specialist post-trauma nurse.

Mum makes suede elbow-gloves for him from chamois leather car cleaning cloths.

Our school won the match by five wickets. Nancy played. She's good.

I groom Rambo before and after school. He can only eat from the eyedropper. He looks miserable. His fur is staring and smelly. It's awful for a cat to not be able to clean himself. They are usually so meticulous about hygiene. Charlie and Flo stay away from him, but what's new?

But then his half-tongue falls off and amazingly he starts to clean himself, licking with his stunted tongue. He licks Bubba's head and face, too, and suddenly he's happy again. On his elbows, toothless, but happy. Another visit to the vet for a check-up. He says he's amazed Rambo has done so well. I was at school when Mum took him this time. His paws are still useless, but he is trying to walk on his leather elbows. He isn't as handsome as he was, of course, and makes a terrible mess when he eats, but his quality of life is improving. Rambo's, I mean, not the vet's.

Mum goes to the car-boot at Hayle on her own while I Rambo-sit. She buys a very elaborate scratching post, but Flo looks at it scornfully and sharpens her claws on the sofa as usual. Bubba comes to visit and Rambo cuddles up to her and licks her head, purring. She falls over onto her back, and he cleans her tummy.

We spend Sunday afternoon at Alistair's cottage. It's looking bright and cheerful with fresh paint. The gulls' sobbing sounds drifting on the wind.

I'm standing on the deck making photographs of the surfers when a peregrine lands on the rail, almost next to me. I'm so surprised I do a loud Oh! And it flies off silently, ghostlike. I'm so stupid. If only I had kept quiet. I think it must have been a young one. That's never happened before. I expect the nest is still on the cliff edge, but I haven't seen the wildlife warden for ages to ask her. I could have taken a close-up of it if I'd kept calm. I could have had it published in *Bird Magazine*. I could have had a reader's letter prize. '*I coulda been a contender.*' Marlon Brando, *On the Waterfront*, 1954.

We go to Mum's favourite beach café and there's a bee on the floor. A wasp buzzes on the window. There are small children in the café so I squash the wasp with my shoe. I show the bee the rose from the jug on our table and it gratefully crawls onto it and I take it outside. When Mum pays she asks for a discount for saving their other diners from stings but they only laugh.

CHAPTER TWENTY-SEVEN

I KNEW HE'D get better! Rambo has the use of his front legs
again. The nerve damage was only temporary, and he is
looking so much better. He still has bald bits, but the fur will
grow back. I'm sure that Bubba has helped his miraculous
recovery. He wants to be fit to look after her. He looks so
noble – his lion profile, his yellow stare!

One of my pocket-money tasks is to groom the cats every
day. I would anyway, but Mum has made it official. It's my
job. I comb Bubba as well, as I don't think Mrs Thomas sees
well enough to do it properly, or she doesn't notice when
Bubba scratches.

Charlie is always the most enthusiastic about being
groomed. When I tap the comb on the outside table she's
always the first to appear. She's so sleek and thick furred and
far bigger than Flo, I think fleas must love her very much. Her
plump body must be to them like our universe is to us. I've
noticed that they gather close to her neck and white throat.
That's where the juiciest ones are. I remove flea dirt from
around her hindquarters. She's a mountainous terrain with
rich valleys. Maybe there are certain parts of her where they
go to breed, other parts where they go to the lavatory and
yet others where they die – like elephants' burial grounds.
She is their world, and when I come along and comb them
out it must be like a hurricane sweeping them away. Some of

them escape of course and live to leap another day, maybe onto a fluffy planet called Rambo or Flo or Bubba.

Another job I have been given this week is to clean out the bathroom cabinets. There are several tiny bottles of hand cream, shampoos, and shower caps from hotels, and I'm suddenly reminded of when I was little and had a toyshop, and Daddy used to give me these sample bottles from his film festival trips. Tiny bars of soap wrapped in pretty paper! Oh, I did like my shop. I had a till with a bell that rang when you opened the drawer to put the money in. Mum kept the miniature bottles of whisky you get on a train for me. Emptied, naturally.

Note: My good deed for the day: I rescue a tiny moth that had got its leg stuck in a fabric loop on a bath-towel. It was struggling and struggling but could not get free. It was a difficult operation. I had to find my magnifying glass and tweezers to extricate him, and he flew away gratefully.

Also I rescued a mouse from Flo, a cricket and another pretty moth. It's colder today and there aren't as many bees finding their way into the house.

More foot metaphors:

Putting my foot in my mouth. Which means saying the wrong thing and getting into trouble because of it.

Putting your right foot forward. Which means starting a project in the correct way, getting started.

Someone at school says that Shiv's mum has stolen lots of money from her employers and has done a bunk to Spain, taking the children with her. And someone else says that her boyfriend is a drug-dealer and a thief and she was scared of getting arrested because of her involvement with him. Who knows? Mum says most gossip is destructive and malicious and I shouldn't listen. Poor Liam, Bridget and Shiv. Even if they wanted to stay here they have to go with their mother.

Maybe when Shiv was being horrid to me when I started school it was because she was being hit at home, and her anger was aimed at me instead of her mum's boyfriend. Mum says that humans are dangerous animals. We can be clever and thoughtful and caring when we are properly brought up, but when we are badly treated and unhappy we can be cruel, destructive and even murderous. If we treat others badly, they will treat others badly and so it goes on...

At the cliff house the storm grows around us. We watch the billowing clouds grow into massive anvils. The sea roars and rushes up the black cliff face. We watch, helpless, from a window as an oiled or exhausted cormorant is smashed again and again on the rocks far below. Its snake-head is searching, searching for a safe landing, but never finds one. I can't bear to watch. He keeps being submerged, dragged down by the waves.

He's not diving, he's drowning.

'Can't we do anything?'

I know we can't. And I feel so miserable and puny. There's nothing I can do in the world to make it a better place, safer from the elements or horrible people.

I have discovered that there was once a rugby team in St Ives made up of eleven men called Stevens. Maybe one of them was a member of my extended family. I must remember to ask Ginnie, if I ever see her again, about her cousins who are Stevens. She said she would introduce me.

We are in Truro shopping for clothes for Mimi's wedding. Mum tries on about a hundred items – suits, dresses, jackets and hats. So-o many hats! I try on four dresses, but hate them all. I know, I shouldn't say hate, it's too strong an emotion, but I would feel happier in my combat gear and I'm sure Willy wouldn't mind. I'm just not a girlie person.

'It's a special occasion and it won't hurt you to make an effort. Do it for Mimi, you know how she loves dressing up.' Mum's word is final.

'Okay, but what about something more interesting?'

'Like what?'

'Vintage.'

'Vintage?'

'Second-hand. Car-boot, antique shop or something.'

'Well, we could look, I suppose.'

'Or I could try on one of your car-boot buys.'

'We'll have a look in my wardrobe when we get home.'

'Okay.'

None of Mum's things fit me, so she and I go to Penzance to look through the second-hand clothes shops and antique shops. I like the middle road there – the spotted horses at Halsetown; a queue of cream cows sheltering from rain under a hedge at Nancledra; the sudden view of St Michael's Mount in Mount's Bay as we go round a sharp bend – like a fairy island in a fantasy movie.

In a retro clothes shop in Chapel Street I find a short kimono jacket – I think it's called a happy coat – in red satin with a black cotton lining. It looks great with jeans but Mum says I can't wear jeans to a wedding, so I compromise with a pair of new black, cropped trousers in cotton, flat red ballerinas and a black T-shirt. I look like a Japanese girl, apart from the hair. Perhaps I could dye it black?

'Yes,' says Mum. '*Très chic*, very Audrey Hepburn.'

'Really?' I turn so I can see myself from behind. Not bad.

Mum has three sets of clothes to choose from. She says she'll make up her mind when she has shown them to Alistair.

'Is he coming to the wedding?'

'He's invited.'

'What about Daddy?'

'He's invited too.'

'Mum, are you going to marry Alistair?'

'He hasn't asked me.'

'But would you if he did?'

'How would you feel if we did?'

I shrug my shoulders. 'Dunno. Okay, I suppose.'

'He is a Very Lovely Man,' says Mum, hugging me.

'Yeah, he's all right. But would I have to change my name to Dobbs? I don't think I could bear that. It's bad enough having the name Augusta!'

'Is that all you're worried about? You would keep your father's name – Stevens.'

'But would you be called Mrs Dobbs?'

'I think I'd like to keep Stevens too. It's a good name. Perhaps I'll be Lara Stevens-Dobbs.' She looks dreamy and young. 'What are we talking about? He hasn't asked me yet.' She laughs and we run across the road carrying our bags of new clothes. I do like my mum. If she married a third time, would she add on the third husband's name too? It could get very silly. Mrs Lara Stevens-Dobbs-Fortescue-Jenkyns-Smythe. Sounds like a person photographed in *Tatler*. They had those in our dentist's waiting room in London. Here they have *Hello!* and *National Geographic*. I hate the dentist even more than I hate the hospital – don't like strangers in my mouth.

Mum tries on all the clothes she bought and doesn't like

any of them in her own mirror. She reckons the mirrors in shops are fixed to make everyone look tall and slender. I would like one of those in my room to make me feel taller. I'm still the smallest girl in my class and the year below. Grandpop said the best things come in small parcels.

Note: Today on the cherry tree in the garden I saw a great tit, blue-tits, a wren, blackbirds, a robin, and an unusual little bird with a chestnut coloured cap, a pale front and brown back and wings. Think it might have been a female blackcap. No male in attendance, though. A pair of canoodling jackdaws balancing on the telegraph wire. One male blackbird on the edge of the water bath sipped then threw his head back and opened his beak. It looked like he was gargling.

'Mum, do you know that only pigeons can drink with their heads down?'

A lot has happened this term. I'm back on the cricket team – going to nets twice a week after school and it's improved my batting and bowling skills.

The mystery of what happened to Bridget and her family is solved. Apparently her mum has been involved in some scam, not for the first time, owed lots of money and left town in a hurry. I think Mum is secretly pleased. She's never approved of my friendship with Siobhan. I miss her, rather – and the excitement of doing things I wouldn't think of doing. I've seen less of Brett lately. He's busy with after-school projects and has made more friends. Hayley is still in Australia looking after her sick mother as far as I know.

Note: Joining the roof gulls this morning – a grey wagtail with yellow front and belly, finding food in the gutter. It's like the hanging gardens of Babylon, full of moss and Aeoniums

*– those prehistoric looking succulents you find on the Scillies
– rather pretty but it needs clearing as it overflows when
it rains. Flo was incensed at the cheeky little bird bobbing
about the other side of the window.*

Today I walked back from school after nets with Nancy and
Emma, and Nancy asked if I would like to have tea at her
house. I phoned Mum and she said yes! Nancy is a really
good fielder, brave and fearless. She's in my class but tall and
strong, the physical opposite of me. She has two hamsters
in a cage and a white rabbit called Peter who runs around
inside the house like a cat. Her dad was there and made
tea for us. She suggests that we toss a ball to each other
across the playing field each lunch break, to strengthen our
throw. We'll only use a tennis ball though, as a cricket ball
could injure an innocent bystander. My aim is good but my
muscles do need building up.

My medication regime is okay but suddenly I'm getting
migraines – wonky vision, shimmering and blind spots. So
annoying. Have to let the hospital know. It's possibly a by-
product of at least one of the drugs I'm taking and they've
suggested taking yet more drugs to help. I have missed
two days' school this week already. I had to be sent home
yesterday morning. My drugs chart reads like a pharmacy
stock report. Charlie came to comfort me in bed, but I
couldn't stand her loud purr and Mum had to remove her.

Back at school. I keep missing stuff and I'm behind in most
subjects.
    Joining an after-school IT class. Brett's in it too. I'm the
only girl out of ten people, but the boys help when I get
stuck. I do love computers. My after-school activities are

more inspiring than in-school work. Mostly because I need extra tuition in basic subjects. I wish Hayley was around so she could give me some home teaching. Brett says his granny has an incurable cancer and is not getting better, and his mum will stay until The End. Maybe they won't be going back to Australia after all? Hayley will come back and they'll carry on living here.

Have another bloody migraine. No school and missed a match at the weekend.

Nancy says it was an ace game and we won. She had two catches in the slips. She's brought us blackcurrants from their garden. Mum's pleased. She phones Nancy's mother to thank her.

Claire brings Gabriel to see me. He's growing up fast, taller than me already, but he's still very sweet. He's being very naughty, Claire says, living in the tree most of the time and only coming down to eat. He's refusing to go to school.

'Why don't you like school, Gabe?'

'Dunno, just don't.'

'What don't you like about it?'

'The work!'

There's no answer to that.

'Are you being bullied?'

'No!'

'Sure?'

'Yeah, I'm sure. I just don't like being there.'

'Well, if you had to stay home and weren't allowed to go to school I bet you'd be desperate to go.'

'Maybe.'

'How are your carnivorous plants?'

'Okay, still eating flies and stuff.'

'I really appreciated when you wrote to me about them when I was in London. It was interesting.'

'Yeah.'

He won't be cheered up. 'Shall I read you a story?'

'No thanks.'

'Would you like to help me with my scrapbook, Gabe?'

'What's a scrapbook?'

'Things I want to keep, like feathers and nature notes and lists of things I like. Drawings and maybe photos of you and your menagerie.'

'Menagerie?'

'Animals.'

'Yeah, okay!'

So we go to Woolworths and I buy a large photo album with clear film that will stick onto the page and keep things in place.

Gabriel draws pictures of all his animals – puppy, floppy-eared rabbits, the tall ducks and chickens and of course Treasure, his cat.

'Will you draw me a carnivorous plant?' He produces a terrifying picture of one eating a huge fly and does a gory picture of his tarantula, Terry the Terrible, being squashed by Troy.

I start making lists of things: favourite movies and movie quotes, family sayings, favourite books, favourite food – that sort of thing. He starts making lists too and wants his own scrapbook.

'Do you have pocket money?' I ask him.

'Yes, but I have to do work for it.'

'That's fair enough, Gabe. So do I.'

'What work do you do?'

'Emptying the dishwasher, hanging out the washing, weeding the patio, tidying my room.'

'I have to clean out the chickens. It's pooey.'

We go back to Woolies on Saturday – his pocket-money day – and he gets a scrapbook like mine. Moss came up with the answer to his school refusing. He pays him to go – 25p per day! He's saving for a microscope. He still gets his ordinary pocket-money too, if he works for it. I wonder if Mum would pay me to go to school? I think it's a brilliant idea. Mum says that women should be paid to stay at home and look after their children, and that way, children wouldn't eat junk food because their mothers would have time to cook proper food, and the children would be brought up properly. Or fathers could be paid to stay at home if their wife had a better job that she didn't want to give up.

'Did you want to keep your job when you had me?'

'No, darling, I wanted to look after you. I was in my forties, don't forget, and you were my first – my only child.' She strokes my spiky hair as if I'm a cat and smiles soppily. 'Anyway you were so ill there was no way I could have gone back to work.'

'Tell me about when I was a baby.' I am cuddling with her on the sofa, Charlie purring and attempting to get in on the act, Flo hanging around on the outskirts of the action, scratching the sofa, Rambo stretched out on the floor. I have heard the stories before, of course.

'I remember when you first walked,' she says. 'The doctors told us you would probably never walk. But you climbed out of your cot at eleven months and banged your head on the side of our tall bed – walked into it.'

'Did it put me off?'

'Not a bit. You were always adventurous.' She smiles.

I haven't heard from Daddy since we were in London for my hospital visit. I ring him.

'Hi, honeybun! How's tricks?'

'I'm fine, thanks. How's the exhibition plans?'

'Nothing final, Guss, nothing fixed yet. But it's a goer, don't worry. These things take time. Still making pictures?'

'Haven't for ages actually. Need more film.'

'See what I can do. What with digital cameras coming in, it's getting harder to get black and white film.'

Digital cameras, mobile phones, laptops – It's all so exciting. All these new things to learn about. I'm lucky to be around when all these inventions are available. I'm lucky to be here at all.

Note: So many little birds in the garden this morning – wren, robin, blackbird, thrush, blackcap, great tit, blue-tit, starling, tree sparrow, dunnock, chaffinch, greenfinch, jackdaw, dove and herring gull. The wren was very close to the window on the garden seat and then searching on the ground in an old grass cutting machine – what for – insects?

CHAPTER TWENTY-EIGHT

A BIG MATCH is coming up and Nancy and I are staying after school all week to practise. Mum says I shouldn't push myself so hard, but it's so wonderful to have the energy, I really feel like it's doing me good, not harm. My throw is better than it was, thanks to training with Nancy every day. There's something very satisfying about hurling a tennis ball over the heads of hundreds of people to reach a small figure on the other side of a field and to be accurate in distance and position. I enjoy catching too, especially when the ball comes in from high up in the sky. It's easier with a cricket ball in fact, as it's heavier and isn't inclined to bounce from your hand like a tennis ball, but we're outlawed from throwing a cricket ball except on the cricket field.

Friday evening – I'm in the nets when I get a migraine. Shit! Call Mum who comes to collect me. I apparently go white. Migraine White – a new colour for my personal colour chart. It's not Brilliant White – more of a grey, beige, blue white, with a hint of mauve. Would be lovely if it was on a wall. On a face it's crap.

Saturday – No way can I play cricket today. It's a forty-eight hour headache, plus the usual trippy visuals – as if I'm on drugs. Well, I know I *am* on drugs, but I mean nonprescription drugs, like LSD or something. Not that I know anything about LSD, but I can't imagine it's much different. Lots of blurry images, jumping colours and fizzy air. Not in a good way.

Can't even listen to nice and gentle voices on Radio Four. Everything hurts my head. All I can do is curl up in bed with a hot water bottle, between trips to the bathroom to talk into the Great White Telephone To God.

Mum bathes my forehead with a damp cloth, as if I've got a temperature. She calls Alistair but he can't help. It's not his expertise – heart and lung transplant aftercare. He's a GP. A family doctor. He's good at finding experts when they are needed for patients with diseases. Good at listening, good at prescribing.

So she phones the hospital and they advise us on what to do. The problem is that if I don't take medication in good time the migraine takes a proper hold and won't be beaten easily.

One good piece of news is that the migraines might be connected to the onset of *periods*! Hurray! I might be showing signs of being normal. Mum goes out and buys me various panty pads just in case. She says she's glad she doesn't have to go through all of that again. Her periods finished when she had her hysterectomy. That means she can't give birth to any more children. She could adopt, I suppose. If she marries Alistair they might want to adopt. I'd like to have a baby brother or sister.

'Mum, would you like to adopt a baby?'

'You've got to be joking!'

'Is that a No, then?'

'Yes, it's a No.'

'I'll definitely adopt, when I'm married. Even if I don't marry.'

'Will you darling? Well, that's marvellous. But I wouldn't be honest if I didn't say it's the hardest job in the world.'

'What is?'

'Looking after a small child. Especially a sick baby.'

'Perhaps you could help me?'

'Wait a bit, eh? A few more years? You haven't started your periods yet. I can't see myself as a grandmother just yet.'

'Okay.'

Remembering the sex education video we had at school, I am not likely to get pregnant in the near future as I don't even want to have sex with anyone I don't actually love. I don't want to get some horrible STD that might stop me having babies in the future. I'll wait until I'm at least eighteen. There's too much to do first – learn, take exams, go to university, think about what I am going to do with the rest of my life.

Possibilities:

1. Photographer
2. Writer (poet; novelist; journalist)
3. Film cameraman (person)
4. Doctor
5. Nurse
6. Naturalist
7. Ornithologist
8. Film Director
9. Professional cricketer.

'Mum, what did you want to be when you grew up?'

'An artist.' She says, drawing a quick sketch of me in charcoal on a large sheet of paper. 'I'll get there yet.'

I go to my bedroom and examine my bumps – can't

really call them breasts yet. But when I stand sideways on
to the mirror there is a definite protrusion, like little limpets.
Yippee, breasts! 'Mum, Mum, I need a bra.'

A new migraine starts as a headache and a strange sort of
thought muddle, where, if I'm relaxing, I get snatches of
conversation coming into my mind, in other people's voices.
Interesting, but I can't remember what they are saying. Like
people in another room. The headache usually starts centrally
and then goes to one temple or the other and often ends up
in one of my back teeth. If I don't take anything at the start
it gets worse and worse and after an hour or so I would be
throwing up every thirty minutes or so for several hours. I
can't think straight at all during all this, simply concentrate
on survival. ENDURE. I have a heavy sort of head for a few
days, and can only eat bland food like tomato soup or Bovril
and dry crackers. Then I have an HFD (headache free day).
    'Did you get migraines before you started your periods?'
    Mum nods her head and holds a wet flannel on my
forehead. 'Poor little darling,' she whispers. 'They'll go
away, don't worry.'

CHAPTER TWENTY-NINE

I'M WATCHING FLO wash herself. She's purring loudly because I have been stroking her. Cats don't have thoughts about the past or the future. They live in the *Now*.

I am hungry. I am thirsty. I am uncomfortable. My fleas are biting. I need a crap.

That's it, simple. Why aren't we like that? Maybe some people are. Humans have such complicated lives compared to cats. Or am I underestimating cats?

Mum had a cat called Gloria who had six sickly kittens – her first litter. She refused to feed them and they died. Gloria was miserable for a year until she had another litter, then she cheered up, purred, was a good mother to her three beautiful kittens. So she must have had thoughts about the past. She was grieving, or perhaps had some chemical in her brain that made her sad. She would sleep all day and not want to play or have anything to do with the other household cats. Definitely depressed.

Cats do remember. And feel jealousy – just watch Charlie and Flo! They have to receive equal attention. Rambo has had more lately, because of his injuries, but he is almost completely recovered. The kitten has learned her place in the hierarchy – third after Flo and Charlie and before Rambo, who always gives way to her.

He is spending more time with us since his accident

and Bubba has practically deserted us for next door and Marigold.

Mum is having jewellery-making lessons with a local professional jeweller. She's having fun, she says, trying new things, learning new skills.

(Kittens learn mew skills!)

We were talking over breakfast – I always want to talk and Mum doesn't want to, she wants to listen to Radio Four, though listening to John Humphrys argue with guests on the *Today* programme seems to make her rather cross. She shouts at the radio. Do other mothers do that?

I find it's the best time to ask the questions she manages to squeeze out of at bedtime. So I asked her about when I was a baby and ill in hospital. And how did she feel when she took me home? And Mum says, 'I was terrified when I took you home. You were kept alive for three months by machines and experts and drugs, and now I was given this little scrap of life and expected to do As Well if not Better. And I had hardly ever Seen a baby let alone Cared for a Sick one.'

'How did you do?'

'Well, you're still here, aren't you?' (I jump up and down and make silly faces to prove that I am still here.) 'But it was difficult, worse than I'd imagined. You were a twenty-four-hours-a-day job, the hardest job in the world. I never slept. You never slept. You cried. But I suspect all babies are hard work – it wasn't just you.' She flattens my spiky hair automatically, as if she wants it to be smoothed down. I push it back up.

'Come on, school!' I reluctantly pick up my backpack full of books and kiss her goodbye.

'Try to enjoy it,' she says as I slam the back gate.

'Yeah, yeah.'

'You forgot your lunch box,' she shouts.

'Ta, Ma,' I reply. I'm a natural poet. If it had been Daddy I'd have said 'Ya, Pa'.

I think about what she said about my babyhood. She reckoned that as I had had such an awful first few months – hurt by needles, operations, pain every time someone picked me up – I had a built-in distrust of everyone, especially her. I wouldn't be comforted. I didn't sleep, but when I did she thought I had died. She would poke me to check I was still alive. It must have been awful for her and Daddy. Except that Daddy used to be away a lot, so escaped the crying and sleepless nights.

CHAPTER THIRTY

Note: Saturday, woken by the loud piercing song of a wren.
Can't see it but it's louder than every other small bird's song.
Loud enough to waken the dead.

I PLAY MUM'S rainforest tape. It's soothing – the sounds of
rain, monkeys, insects, frogs. I am making a recording of
the sounds at Bowling Green – purrs, mews, thumps, clicks,
cars, gulls, voices.

At Peregrine Point the sounds would be of wind and sea,
crows, robins, other song birds, bamboos swishing, surfers
running down the coast path and whooping as they hit a
wave, helicopters, cows, tractors on the distant hill, gulls,
oystercatchers, curlews, palm leaves clapping.

Mum says Nancy can come to breakfast with us. I phone
and tell her to meet us at the café at ten.

She's wearing her cricket gear. Not the pads, naturally.
I'm not playing today but she is.

'The seven item, please,' she says to the waitress, who
looks at me and says:

'The usual Gussie?'

'Please.'

Mum has toast and bacon – I always give her my egg
yolk.

Nancy is impressed that we are obviously regular customers here. Mum gets the *Times and Echo* from under the low table and turns the pages. Nancy and I talk cricket. She's on the team now, not just a reserve. She's big and strong with a good arm. Maybe I'll be like that one day. I eat all my breakfast. I've been dropped from the reserves because I am not reliable.

'That's so unfair!' Nancy fumes. 'You can't help having migraines.'

CHAPTER THIRTY-ONE

I'VE BEEN LOOKING out of my bedroom window at four sailing boats in the bay. I don't think it's a race. Instead, it's a battle against the elements. Squalls and strong gusts race across the flattened water, confusing the sailors and causing havoc. Three of the boats have two people sailing them, one has one person. He has capsized four times at least. I can't watch more than that. I am exhausted watching his efforts to get the boat upright each time. Each time it takes longer. Is he freezing and exhausted? Are his legs like jelly? Is it the first time he has sailed? It looks like it. He doesn't seem to know how to handle a boat, keeps veering into the wind and stopping or going about and tipping over. He has no control of it. The gusts and squalls are hitting him side on and knocking him over, like life does sometimes. And each time you try to right yourself and carry on, it gets harder, not easier. Each blow exhausts you more and makes it harder to start again. Some of the boats are racing along, enjoying the speed, but this one little boat with one sailor is stuck, like a crippled animal trying to cross a swollen river where hungry crocodiles grab him from below and leopards attack from above. At one time three of the boats are sail-down in the water, their crew standing on the centre plate trying to right the boat.

A herring gull sleeps on a ridge of a roof of one of the neighbouring houses, his head tucked under his wing. When I check on him later, he is still asleep but now is standing on one leg, his head tucked under a wing. How does he balance while he sleeps?

CHAPTER THIRTY-TWO

I'M LYING AWAKE at 4.50 a.m. The cats haven't come onto my bed yet. There's rain pattering the window and I can hear one or two gulls calling out over the bay. Being awake when everyone else is asleep is like being given extra time to be alive. I need that extra time as my life will not be as long as most normal healthy people. My advantage is that I know I have a short time to live, so I waste none of it. That doesn't sound like it makes sense, but to me it does. I know what I mean.

I wish Daddy had a female version of Alistair to make him happy. If I get him to take me to hospital he'd meet more nurses. He likes nurses. He flirts with all my nurses given the chance. Katy isn't married. I wonder if Dolores is? I think his problem is that in his job he only gets to meet film industry women, mostly wannabe actresses and models, and it massages his ego to have a leggy lovely by his side for a while, but then he tires of them, because they are usually young and silly or spoilt and are *bears of very little brain*. Mum was his only older woman, she said. She says he doesn't really like strong women. He's too fragile. I haven't met any female doctors on the transplant unit. There's a woman GP in our local primary care practice – Mum's doctor. She's young and good-looking. Perhaps he could meet her somehow.

After breakfast Daddy phones, as if I've conjured him up.

The photography exhibition will be held next January at the London Film Archive. It's definite. Yay!

'When's your next London clinic?' he asks.

'Two weeks time. Will you be there?'

'Sure, I'll be around. You're staying here?'

'Please.'

'I'll take you out for supper.'

'On my own?'

'Your mother can come if she wants to.'

'Malaysian?'

'Yeah, fine. Got to go now, babe, *ciao*!'

He's *still* saying that. He's such a poseur.

Things to look forward to:

1. Mimi's wedding – 5 July
2. My birthday – 11 August
3. Seeing Daddy – two weeks time

Things to dread:

1. Brett leaving – after end of summer term
2. Biopsy – two weeks time
3. Migraines – who knows when?

But why worry? It may never happen, as Grandma used to say.

What if I was born blind instead of with a heart disease? If I walked around St Ives, would I know where I was by the sounds and smells? The wind sings in the wires on the sailing boats parked at the back of The Sloop car park. The Chinese restaurant has an exhaust pipe that lets out cooking smells at the bottom of Barnoon Hill just before the Market Place. The lifeboat house flag smacks in the wind. There's a fresh water stream trickling onto the pebbles the far side of Westcott's Quay. Sea comes up and over onto the walkway by the Arts Club and carries whooshing sand. You can hear the train arrive and leave the station above Porthminster Beach. At Porthmeor the surf is loud and in summer the beach is full of laughter. And in the alley opposite the back door, the smell of bacon cooking every summer morning drifts from the back kitchens of the B&Bs in Atlantic Terrace and there'll always be the cry of the boatman – 'Seal Island, boat leaving for Seal Island.' At least, I hope there will be.

What if I had been born with my heart problems in a black township in South Africa or in starving Zimbabwe now? I wouldn't survive long. At least Presh had his chance of a transplant.

What if I had died when I was a baby? Would Mum have had another child? Probably not, as she was so old. Maybe she would have adopted. Maybe she would have died of sorrow. What if I had been born with a normal heart and normal everything else? Would I be the same person or has my heart condition made me who I am?

What if Daddy was still living with us. What if I hadn't searched for Daddy's family – we would still know the Darlings, but we wouldn't know that we were related.

I have been rereading the letters from Natalie's mother. I want to meet them, I really do. When I asked Mum what she thought about it she said it was up to me entirely, but if I want to invite them here I can.

Though they might not want to come. Or perhaps I could go there.

I would like to meet Natalie's mother and her brothers.

She didn't mention a father. Maybe there isn't one. Or maybe he's like mine – absent, invisible, divorced, separated, or dead.

Maybe we could meet on neutral ground, no-man's land, somewhere halfway between both our homes. But she hasn't written to me for ages and I haven't written to her. I wonder if she thinks about me? She must do. When I die, her daughter's heart and lungs will, after all, perish with me. It might be like her daughter's death all over again.

CHAPTER THIRTY-THREE

THE BIOPSY GOES as well as it can do – horrid sensations, soreness afterwards.

We discuss my migraines and what to do about them. The doctor says that they might well go away once my periods start, but to take the prescribed medications at the first sign. He'll review the situation at my next visit. My immunosuppressants are doing what they are supposed to do. I don't see anyone I know in the clinic.

The transplant co-ordinator comes out of her office as we are passing.

'Gussie, how are you, dear?'

I tell her about Natalie and her mother's letters.

Mum says, 'Do you think it would be a good idea to meet her, or not?'

'Come in to the office for a minute,' Miss Aphra holds the door open. 'I have seen several get-togethers between recipients and donor families. If and when you and she are ready, I'd go for it. It's a strange relationship, but can prove very valuable and rewarding for all concerned.'

'Have you met Mrs Bridges?' asks Mum. I can see that she's dubious about the whole thing. I know what she means. We might not like them. It could be very difficult. They might stalk me or something.

'She's a delightful woman. I can't say more than that.'

'Could you organise it, please?' I ask her.

'If you want me to, but if you've already got her email address, why not ask her directly?'

We had dinner out with Daddy the night before at my favourite restaurant – Malaysian food – hot, sweet, sour, yummy. Shame I can't have the shellfish. My favourite is the sticky flat bread and the flat rice noodles with all sorts of goodies in it – pork, chicken, veggies, prawns (I have to remove the prawns.) Daddy didn't bring Ilenya, his Rumanian actress-girlfriend. Mummy and he were almost civilised to each other except for one moment when she flew off the handle.

'I might be getting married again,' she said.

'The quack?'

'Mmm.'

'Must you?'

'What do you mean?'

'Well, why can't you just live together?'

'I like the security of marriage.'

'Huh!'

'Well, you wouldn't understand. You never kept your vows.'

'Huh, vows mean nothing.'

'They do. They don't mean anything to you, maybe, but they do to people who live in the real world.'

'What do you know about the real world? You don't have to work.'

'What do *you* know about the real world? You live in a fantasy world.'

They were getting louder and louder. I say, 'You're giving me a headache, do you mind?' And amazingly they shut up.

'Invitations,' says Daddy.

'What?'

'Mailing list. Give me a mailing list for the exhibition.
People you want to come to the view.'

'Oh, will there be a party?'

'Sort of – drinks, anyway. Just an hour or two.'

'Will it be in term-time?'

'You'll have to take time off if it is.'

I do like the train journey there and back. In West Cornwall
there aren't many trees, so you can't tell what the seasons are
doing. I prefer winter trees, when the skeletons are visible
and the bones of the land, but now the leaves are a tired
grey-green, dusty and old. There aren't many birds, only a
few crows, a brilliant pheasant or two standing in a ploughed
field, the usual fleet of swans drifting by the pier under the
Isambard Kingdom Brunel Bridge. The train is full and this
time we are in a Standard Class quiet carriage – except it's
very noisy with small children running up and down.

'Did I run up and down the carriage when I was little,
Mum?'

'You once walked all the way from Cornwall to London.
I was exhausted.'

'How old was I?'

'Two, I think. We had been staying in a guest house in
Looe for a week. It was hell. You cried every night. It was
no holiday.'

'Sorry Mum,' I apologise. She hugs me to her.

'I forgive you.'

CHAPTER THIRTY-FOUR

THE WEDDING OF the Year!

We're staying at Daddy's place. He's not here because he's staying at his girlfriend's place. Haven't met her yet but she's coming to the wedding. Mum has brought her entire summer wardrobe, or that's what it looks like. I have one small suitcase on wheels and a backpack. She made me leave my binoculars and bird books in Cornwall. Urgh!

Alistair won't be here for the wedding, he's at work. It'll be the first time I've been to London for anything other than a hospital appointment. I won't know anyone apart from Mum, Dad, Mimi and Willy. I expect it'll be boring but what can I do? I'm here for Mum.

Daddy told me I looked like a young Audrey Hepburn – hmm. I thought she looked rather anorexic in *Breakfast at Tiffany's*. I have had my hair trimmed specially, so has Mum. He kisses Mum and tells her she looks gorgeous and he wishes he hadn't left her.

'I left you actually,' she reminds him.

Oh no, not a row at Willy and Mimi's wedding! Luckily he goes off to kiss some other woman. I think he kisses every woman there.

Surprise – I know lots of people. The French Connection, one of Mum's and Mimi's old work friends. And all of Willy's allotment friends who I met ages ago. It's a lovely party. Ilenya is not happy. She slaps Daddy around the face because he kissed Mum for rather too long.

'He always was a good kisser,' says Mum.

I don't think she'll last – Ilenya.

Mimi looks voluptuously Italian in a cream silk suit, a low-necked frilly top and red high-heels, but I think she's had something done to her face. Her lips look odd, sort of bloated as if she's got an allergy, but Willy looks proud in a cream linen and silk jacket, navy silk shirt and dark trousers. He wears a navy silk cravat.

'Not a day over sixty,' says Mum to him.

'I feel not a day over fifty,' he says gleefully.

'How old is he, anyway?'

'Eighty-two, he admits to. So probably eighty-five.'

I am the only child guest. I do have my camera, so I spend a lot of time making portraits of the guests. The party is in the garden behind Willy and Daddy's flats. It's warm and sunny. I think about how I found Beelzebub on the doorstep in the rain. And I check out the bird-feeders – empty! Daddy is useless at birds – both kinds.

'Can't see the attraction to Ilenya, Pa,' I say.

'Whatya mean? She's stunning,' he says, throwing back another glass of bubbly.

'So?'

'And passionate,' he says, stroking his sore cheek and grinning.

'So?'

'Wait till you fall in love, Gussiebun.'

I wish I were on the Island in St Ives, in comfortable combat gear, Brett lying next to me, gulls' cries in my ears, the scent of salt air, granite behind me, waves battering the rocks, perhaps a seal's head bobbing, whiskers dripping diamonds.

'Daddy. Don't you want to fall in love for ever and ever?'

'I'm always in love. But you I'll love forever,' he says. I believe him.

Mimi shows us her ring. It looks pretty ordinary to me, but Mum Oohs and Aahs over it. She still wears all her other rings – the diamonds, rubies, emeralds and opals she has been given by ex-husbands and lovers. I love her shoes, which are bright red, high-heeled and with a peep toe, and low at the sides so you can see the instep. Perhaps I'll be a fashion designer, a shoe designer. A designer of something.

I drink half a glass of champagne and immediately get a migraine. Shit! There are classic migraine triggers: coffee – I don't drink coffee. Chocolate. Cheese. Red wine. I don't usually drink wine. And champagne is white. Buggering Nora, is all I have to say. I disappear into Daddy's bedroom and stay there, and Mum attends to me. Wish he still had a black mosquito net over the bed. I need a thick black net over my eyes. The sound of people having fun is too loud. Everything is too loud.

When I'm better, the jollities are all over and Mum takes me back to Cornwall. Didn't see Daddy much. Mimi and Willy have gone on honeymoon to Italy, where some of her relations live. Most of them are in Australia, where she used to live. I would love to go to Australia. With Brett maybe one day? Can't wait to get back to normality, the cats, bird-watching, school. Well, maybe not school... my room, Alistair. I give up with Daddy. He's not ready for a full-time commitment to anyone. He might never be ready. Mum's ready, I reckon.

Am I ready for a new father?

CHAPTER THIRTY-FIVE

Note: A kenning (derived from the Old Norse) is a compound poetic phrase used instead of the name of a person or thing, expressing something in terms of another – 'whale road' for sea or 'word hoard' for book. 'Railroad' is a kenning.

I HAVE A new word – kenning. My kennings:

> hawk road – sky
> worm road – soil
> cloud road – sky
> thought hoard – journal
> clothes hoard – Mum's wardrobe
> image hoard – camera

I am keeping a journal and still trying to write poems. I want to write about Rambo. He is so stoic and uncomplaining. He still limps but is able to clean himself (sort of) and eat (messily) but his quality of life is good. He purrs when he's groomed and when he grooms (slobbers over) Bubba. He enjoys lying in the sun, lying on his back with his legs in the air, Greek yoghurt.

Mum is getting me some extra tuition at home again with Steve (Brett's dad) – he teaches Maths. I'm glad. I panic about being left behind.

I go to the car-boot with Mum. I buy sunflower seeds and peanuts. Mum buys veggies and plants, even though there's no more room in the tiny garden for even a daisy.

'I'll make room,' she says.

'Brett's here to see you,' Mum shouts up to me.

'Send him up.'

'Howya doin?'

'Yeah, good, you?'

'Good, thanks.'

Why can't we talk to each other? He doesn't look good. He's sad, I can tell. His curly mouth droops at the edges and he won't look at me. Is he going back to Australia sooner than he thought?

'You all right, Brett?'

'Yeah, I suppose. It's my gran. She died.'

'Oh, I'm sorry.'

I think he's going to cry. If anyone ever shows me sympathy when I'm sad, it makes *me* cry.

'Is your mum very upset?'

'She phoned last night. I think she's relieved it's all over.'

'Is she coming back or what?'

'She didn't say. There's the funeral first.'

'Will you go?'

'It's a long way to go for a funeral.'

'But are you all going to stay in England?'

'Dunno. It's up to Mum.'

'Want to go birding?'

'Nah.' He smiles his curly smile. 'Not much around this time of year.'

'Oh, okay. What shall we do, then?'

Mum saves us from indecision. 'Would you like to stay

for lunch, Brett?' she shouts up the stairs.

'Thanks, Mrs Stevens,' he shouts back. 'Smells good,' he says. 'Dad doesn't cook much.' Poor Brett, he's missing his mum. Being Sunday, we have roast chicken, roast potatoes, peas and beans and a green salad, followed by fresh fruit. Brett eats seconds. Mum likes having people to feed. Alistair isn't around today.

'What's your father doing today?' she asks.

'Oh, he's working in the garden. He doesn't do lunch.'

After the meal we go up to the attic and look out of the window at the gulls. The adults are asleep. There's one backward young gull still on the roof, hunched shoulders, wheezing. I feel sorry for his parents, still having this big ugly teenager demanding food all the time. A bit like Charlie, who's always hungry and wants to be fed ten times a day. Brett is holding a war-torn but happy Rambo on his lap and stroking his neck. Lucky Rambo.

'Brett, I'm in touch with my organ donor's family.'

'Yeah? When are you going to meet them?'

'Do you think I should?'

'Sure. I would. It's more family, isn't it? They would be like family, I should think.' He picks up a feather and starts to tickle me under the chin with it. We end up giggling and play fighting on the floor, the cats outraged at our behaviour.

I hadn't realised that he was so sensitive to my feelings about family. He's so nice, gorgeous, wonderful, sensitive, hunky, and I do love him.

Note: Monday. A small tragedy for the bird life in our garden: I came in after school to find fluffy feathers all over the sitting room and a very dead chaffinch under a chair. No sign of the murderer. The cats were all asleep, pretending to be innocent. I spent ages hoovering it all up and threw out the corpse. But later more feathers appeared from nowhere. Mum keeps singing 'Falling in love again, never wanted to, what am I to do? I can't help it,' in a sexy German accent. She says she's being Marlene Dietrich, a German actress during the Second World War.

Why are there so many wars?

Everywhere in the world, it seems, people are killing each other, because they can't agree about their gods or their government. But if there were no wars there would be too many people. It's one way of keeping the numbers down, and as there are far too many people being born for the Earth to provide for, I suppose war is one sure way of lowering the population figures. That and disease, drought, floods, earthquakes, volcanoes, etc.

I should have died when I was born, and would have died if I had been born in a poorer country. Survival of the fittest – Darwin. I'm glad I didn't.

Mum says my life is precious and important. I bring joy to her and Daddy, she says. Also, I intend to do something meaningful with my life. Not sure yet what it will be. I have already saved the life of Siobhan, so that's something. Or it will be, if she manages to do something worthwhile with her life. I wonder where she is, and what's she doing. I miss her little sister more than her: dear little Bridget with her colourful emotions.

Perhaps I'll be a doctor, or a firefighter.

I am marking time until I hear from Brett if he's staying in England or going back to Australia. I can't settle to anything. School is a drag. I spend lunch break throwing a ball, the highlight of my day. I have made up my mind. I do want to meet Abigail Bridges and her sons. I email her:

Dear Mrs Bridges,

I would like very much to meet you and your children if you are agreeable. If and when you are ready to meet, we could see you in Scotland or meet here, or wherever you wish. Here is our telephone number. I do hope you want to meet.

Best wishes,
Gussie

I sort of hoped she'd reply straight away, but she doesn't. Maybe she's one of those people who only look at her emails once a week, like Mum. I look every day, though it's only Brett and Gabriel who email me. Brett's messages are usually about birds or plants and Gabe's are about carnivorous plants. Nancy is getting a computer of her own soon, which will be great. I do like her. She's the opposite of me – she's as strong as a boy and I'm puny, apart from my good throwing arm.

I'm not the only one at after-school Maths tuition. Nancy is having problems (probs, in Australian) too. A couple of boys – Bas and Matt – are also in the class. It's interesting. I think I am beginning to understand about numbers and their significance at last. Brett is good at Maths. I suppose it's inherited. He's pretty good at everything he does, except sports, which he despises. I wish he'd come and watch me play cricket. I'm in the reserves again, due to two of the girls being unfit. Yippee! I mean, it's a shame they aren't well, but, there you go, it's their turn. I've had enough illness. I want to be well and healthy and fit and strong and brilliant at cricket.

Mum, Nancy and I watch Alistair play cricket and while

he is waiting to bat I bowl to him. Nancy says I'm improving greatly. The match is played on our school field, surrounded by mature oaks and other trees I don't know the names of. I'm no good at trees. We lie on a blanket and Mum drinks wine. It's a perfect summer's day, warm and sunny, but with a breeze coming off the bay. Two military planes go over, close together, like a pair of companionable gulls. Swallows swoop low over the grass, flashing blue. No horses run in the field below the cricket field today. We watch Alistair bat – he got twenty-eight runs, then Nancy and I go off to the nets to practice. I have loads of bruises on my legs from the ball. I'm rather proud of them. The thing is not to complain when you get hit. Be brave. Our school team is doing really well in the Cornwall Schools' league. There's a big match coming up soon and I want to play in it.

Opal, who is a really good medium-fast bowler, is one of the girls who is ill. She has glandular fever and won't be back for weeks. Taylor has a broken arm (she fell off her skateboard) and will be off the team for the rest of the summer term. She's an all-rounder. I have been in the nets every day, and when we have PE I get loads of praise for my improvement. I really want to play against Goldsithney boys.

I'm in the team, it's official! My name is up there on the board with Josephine as captain. Nancy's in, too. We jump up and down like idiots, whooping and yelling. Brett comes by at that moment and looks amazed.

'I'm in. I'm on the team,' I tell him.

'Righto, rippa!' He tries to smile for me, but I can see that he hasn't really got his heart in it (another heart metaphor).

I'm going with Nancy and her dad. He's one of the umpires.

'Don't you want me to watch?' Mum asks.

'Of course. Bring Alistair if you want.'

'Thanks, I might do that.'

My Maths lesson after school is a drag. I want to be out on the field, practising my bowling. But I manage to get through it without too much dreaming. Steve is looking bedraggled and scruffy. I don't think he's any good at looking after Brett or himself. Useless men! They need Hayley to come back.

I persuade Mum to invite them for lunch on Sunday with Alistair.

ALISTAIR:	'How's things, Steve?'
STEVE:	'Yeah, no worries.'
MUM:	'When's Hayley coming home?'
STEVE:	'There's the question. I don't know. She won't say.'
MUM:	'I suppose there's lots to do, clearing her mother's things?'
STEVE:	'So I believe, yeah.'

I get the feeling he doesn't want to talk about it; there's more to it than Hayley's mother's death. Perhaps she wants to stay there. Perhaps she doesn't want to be with Steve any more. My parents split up. I know loads of people whose parents have split up. Brett is quiet too.

'How's my daughter's Maths coming along?' Mum asks.

'Yeah, no worries, she'll be fine.' That's one good thing, anyway. I haven't had a migraine for a week or so, either. I'm praying I won't get one before the MATCH.

I have bought my first bra (two to be exact, one to wear, one to wash). It's the smallest bra in the world, but it's a start. At least I won't be aware of bouncing bumps when I'm bowling.

That's alliteration – all those Bs.

Note: A huge pool has been formed in the harbour area by a sandbank, and loads of little fish – sprats, sand eels? – get stuck in it, causing huge flocks of gulls to congregate and glut on the trapped shoals. It's marvellous that they don't all crash into one another when they dive. They must have excellent radar. I make some photographs of them and take the film to the Times and Echo *office, but they already have their own.*

'No rescues lately then?' the editor asks me. I smile scathingly and don't deign to answer such a silly question.

'I'm having a photo exhibition actually, in London,' I brag, and wish I hadn't as soon as the words are out. Knowing Daddy as I do, it might not happen, even though he says it definitely will. And how embarrassing would that be? Anyway, it's not cool to promote one's self. Or is it oneself?

'Well, when you do, let us know and we'll give you a plug.'

'A plug?'

'Tell people about it.'

'Oh, would you? Thanks.' I'll be able to put it in my scrapbook with the other newspaper clippings. I've got so much stuff in there now. It's the sort of thing to do when the weather's bad or when I'm unwell. Where did the expression 'give you a plug' come from?

CHAPTER THIRTY-SIX

THE BIG MATCH. It's the first time we've played against a boys-only team. They are all thirteen or under, but big. Much bigger than most of us, and stronger, I expect. We are in the visitors' changing room, excited and nervous. We're fielding first.

The home team has loads of support – enthusiastic crowds of boys and parents. We have parents and a few friends. Mum and Alistair are sitting on the grass with a bottle of champagne. Claire and Gabe join them. I try not to wave but keep smiling in their direction.

I get to field out on the boundary at mid-wicket. It's warm and humid. My glasses are slipping down my nose. A black-headed gull (or is it a tern?) gleans the grass nearby. Oops! Mustn't bird watch while I'm fielding. So many balls come my way. I'm kept busy running here and there and everywhere. I'm glad to have had all that practice throwing with Nancy. I can throw really hard now. Jo is brilliant. She's got three wickets. She runs in to bowl to their best bat – he's been in since the start. Samson. I don't know if that's his first name or his surname. It suits him. I think of the old movie *Samson and Delilah*. Where he pulls down the stone pillars on top of himself. She bowls a straight ball and he hits it straight back. But when she tries to catch it she goes over on her ankle and collapses. It goes for four. Shit!

Jo, our captain, our best player, limps off, injured. Lisa is now captain. She runs to me.

'You bowl. Give it your best.'

'Me?'

'Yeah, just do it, okay?'

'Okay!' We do a high five and I do a practice bowl or two with Nancy catching. It feels great, this. I can run. I can use my muscles. I'm fit, healthy, normal, like everyone else. It feels so good. Then the anxiety comes. Will I be able to do this? Am I up to it? Will I let down my team? I have to do it right. And then I remember my grandpop saying to me as I leaped from beach hut roof to roof at Shoeburyness, 'You can do it, Princess, you can do it.'

And I do it. I bowl my best balls ever – yorkers, line and length spinners, outside off stump, but nothing I do is good enough to get a wicket. Goldsithney are scoring fast. Nancy and I bowl in tandem. She gets a wicket. High fives all round. Samson's still there, huge, indomitable. I'm into it now, and the ball's beginning to turn. I do a short run up, and turn my wrist, so. A perfect Chinaman. Samson lifts his bat too early, expecting a faster ball and his middle stump comes out of the ground. The marble pillars fall and he is vanquished. Or that's what it feels like.

The whole field erupts in cheers and I'm lifted high by several girls. I blush with pleasure and embarrassment. I'm a hero – heroine. A new batsman comes onto the field. But Samson had been the best man. We bowl out the others before the twenty overs are done – all out for ninety-five. Will we be able to beat that score?

As I walk off with the others, I see him – Brett! And his mum and dad, holding hands. She's back! Mum and Alistair are applauding loudly. I can't help grinning like mad. We have tea in the pavilion, girls on one table, the boys, subdued, whispering, on the other. Jo has a cold compress on her ankle and looks pale, but sits with us to talk about the order of batting. We're one bat down, of course, with Jo injured. I'm to be number eleven as I'm the youngest and newest member of the team. Lisa's captain now, but she defers to Jo about the order of play. We just have time to go out and talk to our supporters before a quick wee and then our first batters get their pads on. Lisa and Opal open the batting. We get sixty runs for six wickets. Not looking good. We just about scrape through to eighty for nine, Lisa is still there, and she's the only one getting runs. We aren't used to facing such fast balls. It's embarrassing.

I am padded up and in terror. Kelly is out for a duck and it's me. Where's my bat? I can't find it. Jo hands me hers and smiles encouragingly. It's a long walk out to the centre.

'You can do it Gussie,' shouts Mum (or maybe Grandpop, I can't be sure). Lisa comes to meet me.

'Don't try to score. Just defend the wicket. I can do the scoring.'

I manage to put my bat in the right place and keep out a stunning yorker. Our team cheer every ball that I keep out.

Last ball of the over. I'm safe.

Lisa hits the first ball of the next over for a boundary. Jubilation all round. The bowler's a small, slim boy with an odd action, but he's good. He's got five of the eight wickets. We run two, then another two. We need another run to get Lisa down the right end so she can bat the last over. But something goes wrong. I find myself facing the fast bowler, Samson – him again! How many runs do we need? Five to draw, six to win. The first is a dot ball. I'm sweating madly. Terrified I'll let down the side. At least I'm surviving, though the ball hits my gloved hand and my thumb hurts like mad. I take off my glove to have a look.

Lisa strolls down to me and says – 'We can do this. Just get me up your end.'

I can still move my thumb, so it's not broken. I put my glove on again and take up my stance. His run up is fast and furious, but he bowls slightly short and wide. I hit it! Too high! An outfielder goes to catch it, but he misses and the ball rolls to the boundary. A four, I've got a boundary! Everyone cheers and claps.

I push my glasses up my slippery nose and take up my position again, remembering to relax, to keep my eye on the ball all the way to the bat. My thumb hardly hurts at all. I am calm, focused. I can do this!

I miss the ball but it goes past the keeper and Lisa shouts, 'Run!'

One of my pads comes loose and I fall over it, staggering the last couple of metres, hurling myself down and stretching my bat to get in. I make it! The ground is loud with cheers and whoops. The umpire hands me my glasses and I adjust the pads and make sure they are on tight.

The scores are even; we need one run to win.

The last ball in the game belongs to Lisa. Samson takes a long run up and bowls with venom, a bouncer. But Lisa is ready for it. She gives herself lots of room and hits the ball in the middle of the bat, behind her, and the crowd screams with joy as it goes over the boundary without hitting the ground. A six!

We run to each other and hug and then shake hands with the umpires and the members of the other team and Lisa and Nancy lift me onto their shoulders and carry me off. I'm in a haze of happiness. What joy to be part of a winning side, with everyone clapping like mad. Brett is grinning and clapping, Steve and Hayley are hugging each other and looking happy. Mum and Alistair, Claire and Gabe are cheering me off the field. I don't think I've ever been so happy. Jo hugs me and says, 'Well done Gussie,' and takes her bat and kisses it. Mrs Payne tells me I did brilliantly. I wish Daddy had been here to see me, and wouldn't Grandpop and Grandma have been proud!

But best of all, Brett hugs me in front of all my team and says, 'You were rippa, Guss,' and smiles his curly smile.

'Are you staying in England?' I ask.

'Yeah, I reckon.'

I suddenly become aware of another person standing with Mum and Alistair. It's a large, round black woman almost bursting out of a bright floral dress and wearing a straw hat with flowers around the brim. She's smiling broadly.

I know without being told that it's Natalie's mother. I'm speechless.

'Gussie, this is Mrs Bridges.'

We fall into each other's arms, tears wetting our cheeks.

'Your mother said to come this weekend. I hope it's not too big a shock,' she says. She hugs me to her huge, soft bosom.

'Thank you, thank you,' is all I can say.

'Those are my boys,' she says, still holding me, and pointing to two lads in the nets, one bowling to the other.

'I am so glad to meet you,' she says, and her hand is pressed to my heart, feeling the steady pump and beat of my blood.

The Burying Beetle

Ann Kelley

ISBN 1 84282 099 0 PBK £9.99

ISBN 1 905222 08 4 PBK £6.99

The countryside is so much scarier than the city. It's all life or death here.

Meet Gussie. Twelve years old and settling into her new ramshackle home on a cliff top above St Ives, she has an irrepressible zest for life. She also has a life-threatening heart condition. But it's not in her nature to give up. Perhaps because she knows her time might be short, she values every passing moment, experiencing each day with humour and extraordinary courage.

Spirited and imaginative, Gussie has a passionate interest in everything around her and her vivid stream of thoughts and observations will draw you into a renewed sense of wonder.

Gussie's story of inspiration and hope is both heartwarming and heartrending. Once you've met her, you'll not forget her. And you'll never take life for granted again.

Gussie fairly fizzles with vitality, radiating fun and enjoyment into everything that comes her way. Her life may be predestined to be short but not short on wonder, glee, the love of things as they really are. It is rare to find such tragic circumstances written about without an ounce of self-pity. Rarer still to have the story of a circumscribed existence escaping its confines by sheer force of personality, zest for life.

MICHAEL BAYLEY

The Bower Bird
Ann Kelley
ISBN 1 906307 98 9
(children's fiction) PBK £6.99
ISBN 1 906307 45 8
(adult fiction) PBK £6.99

I had open-heart surgery last year, when I was eleven, and the healing process hasn't finished yet. I now have an amazing scar that cuts me in half almost, as if I have survived a shark attack.

Gussie is twelve years old, loves animals and wants to be a photographer when she grows up. The only problem is that she's unlikely to ever grow up.

Gussie needs a heart and lung transplant, but the donor list is as long as her arm and she can't wait around that long. Gussie has things to do; finding her ancestors, coping with her parents' divorce, and keeping an eye out for the wildlife in her garden.

Winner of the 2007 Costa Children's Book Award

It's a lovely book – lyrical, funny, full of wisdom. Gussie is such a dear – such a delight and a wonderful character, bright and sharp and strong, never to be pitied for an instant.

HELEN DUNMORE

Luath Press Limited

committed to publishing well written books worth reading

LUATH PRESS takes its name from Robert Burns, whose little collie Luath (*Gael.*, swift or nimble) tripped up Jean Armour at a wedding and gave him the chance to speak to the woman who was to be his wife and the abiding love of his life. Burns called one of the 'Twa Dogs' Luath after Cuchullin's hunting dog in Ossian's *Fingal*. Luath Press was established in 1981 in the heart of Burns country, and is now based a few steps up the road from Burns' first lodgings on Edinburgh's Royal Mile. Luath offers you distinctive writing with a hint of unexpected pleasures.

Most bookshops in the UK, the US, Canada, Australia, New Zealand and parts of Europe, either carry our books in stock or can order them for you. To order direct from us, please send a £sterling cheque, postal order, international money order or your credit card details (number, address of cardholder and expiry date) to us at the address below. Please add post and packing as follows: UK – £1.00 per delivery address; overseas surface mail – £2.50 per delivery address; overseas airmail – £3.50 for the first book to each delivery address, plus £1.00 for each additional book by airmail to the same address. If your order is a gift, we will happily enclose your card or message at no extra charge.

Luath Press Limited

543/2 Castlehill
The Royal Mile
Edinburgh EH1 2ND
Scotland
Telephone: +44 (0)131 225 4326 (24 hours)
Fax: +44 (0)131 225 4324
email: sales@luath. co.uk
Website: www. luath.co.uk